WINTER AT CHRISTMAS INN

A SWEET SMALL TOWN CHRISTMAS ROMANCE

ANNE-MARIE MEYER

D1450414

Copyright © 2019 by Anne-Marie Meyer

All rights reserved.

No part of this book may be reproduced in any form or by any electronic or mechanical means, including information storage and retrieval systems, without written permission from the author, except for the use of brief quotations in a book review.

For my Family

HOLLY

Rex Potter sat across from Holly, tapping his fingers on his desk. She watched him as his eyes roved over the stack of papers he had in front of him.

He let out a few harrumphs before he again grew silent.

Holly bounced her leg, silently begging him to move forward with the reading of the will.

This was not where she wanted to be. She'd just buried her grandmother—the woman she swore she would never talk to again—and she was more than ready to forget her past and every painful memory that lay there.

Rex's instance to read over the will once more was killing her.

She had half a mind to fire her lawyer—but he was the best New York had to offer. And her boyfriend's father. And then there was the fact that he'd agreed to look over the will for free.

"I really don't see a way out of this, Holly. I mean, it's the only way for you to move on from Christmas Inn. If you want to sell it—"

"I do," Holly blurted out as heat crept up her cheeks. Having this inn hanging over her head was slowly crushing her. Selling it meant that she could once and for all shed her past and move forward.

Rex glanced over his readers at her, his greying mustache twitching as he studied her. Then he glanced at the papers as he set them down on the desk and sighed. "Then you have to spend this Christmas at the inn. There's no way around it."

Holly's stomach twisted at Rex's resolute words. She parted her lips to speak, but from the no-nonsense look in his eyes, she knew that resistance was futile. If there was a way to get out of it, Rex would have found it.

There was nothing she could do.

She was going to have to return to Ivy Springs. Return to the Christmas Inn she'd fled ten years ago. The moment she'd been able to get out of that god-forsaken town and away from her grandmother, she had. And she hadn't looked back.

Holly took a deep, cleansing breath as she nodded. "Thanks, Rex." She leaned down and grabbed her purse, which she had set beside her chair. "I'll think about it."

Rex nodded as he moved to stand. "I really think it's best. And honestly, the land is appraising for three million dollars. Quite a nice nest egg if you ask me."

Holly almost swallowed her tongue. Three million was quite a lot. Enough, in fact, for her to dig herself out of her mounting debt and create her own line of women's fashion—something that she'd been dreaming of since she was little.

She could make something of herself. Prove that she wasn't just some Podunk kid from the middle of Massachusetts. She was born to be something more.

Extending her hand, Holly nodded. "Thanks."

Rex met her handshake and narrowed his eyes. "Talk it over with Tyler. See what he thinks. And who knows, maybe some time in the country might be good for you two."

Not wanting to discuss her and Tyler's relationship, Holly just smiled and slipped on her coat. "I will. I'm meeting him tonight for drinks. We can discuss it then."

Rex nodded and then motioned toward the door. "Let me know as soon as you decide. A week at Christmas Inn during the holiday season is all you need to do to fulfill the stipulation. Once that's over, you can sell and move on."

Holly moved to his office door and pulled it open. Just before she stepped out into his waiting area, Rex called out to her once more.

"There was one more thing. The will said something about a Stephen Jones? Does that name ring any bells with you?"

Holly stopped at the mention of Stephen's name. Her hand felt frozen as it rested on the doorknob. She should have known her grandmother would include Stephen. After all, she'd basically raised him alongside Holly.

He was part of the past she was trying to forget. A love she'd shoved way down in her memory since the day he broke her heart. She'd sworn she would never think of Stephen or the Christmas Inn again, yet here she was, doing both.

"What about him?" she asked, turning slowly. Rex stood behind his desk with his mustache twitching as he studied a piece of paper.

"It says that Stephen Jones is entitled to 10 percent of the inn or the proceeds from its sale." He glanced up at Holly. "You know him?"

Muscling down the heartache that was trying to suffocate her, Holly swallowed hard and nodded. "When I sell the inn, I'll reach out to Stephen. Easy peasy."

Rex nodded, and Holly turned back around, ready to get out of this room and away from the bad memories the will had dredged up. She was ready to move on with her life.

Talia, her assistant, was sitting on one of the overstuffed armchairs that lined the far wall of the waiting room. She was busy talking on her phone, oblivious to the fact that Holly was ready to leave.

Talia was ditzy and goofy, but Holly couldn't help but keep Talia as her assistant. She'd grown to love her frizzy blonde hair and bight, blue eyes. She was spontaneous and cheerful, which were qualities that Holly's life sorely lacked.

"Come on, we're done here," Holly said as she tapped Talia's black heels with her own red ones.

Talia's face flushed as she glanced up. She pulled the phone from her cheek and hit the end call button. "I'm so sorry," she said as she shoved the phone into her purse. "I just..." She winced. "Holiday family planning in the works."

Holly chuckled despite the familiar ache that rose up inside of her at the mention of the holiday season. She'd walked away from all that merriment years ago. When she'd found out her grandmother had lied to her. When she found out the real reason her mother had left her, never to be seen again. Add in her breakup with Stephen, and if she never saw a Christmas tree or smelled mulled apple cider again, it would be too soon.

She'd renounced Christmas and everything that had to do with this time of year.

"It's okay," she said as she pulled out her gloves and slipped them on. December in New York City had a way of chilling you to the bone. After tightening her scarf around her neck, she waited for Talia before she pushed the outer door and stepped out onto the bustling sidewalk.

Just as the door shut behind them, she heard Rex's desperate voice.

"Wait!" he shouted as he burst out after them.

Confused, Holly turned around to see a white envelope that he clutched in his hand. Rex's face was red from exertion as he hunched over, taking in deep breaths.

"Did I forget something?" Holly asked.

Rex straightened and held out the envelope. "A letter. It came with the will. It's addressed to you."

He waved it under Holly's nose. She studied it for a moment, a war being waged inside of her. Did she take it? Did she wanted to know what it said?

There was only one person who could have included a letter with the will.

Her grandmother.

But reading the dying words of Hope Graham wasn't something she wanted to do. The apology that she was pretty sure was written in that letter wasn't one she wanted to hear.

Things happened. And there was nothing anyone could do to change the past. Lives had been irrevocably changed because her grandmother had felt she knew best.

Well, Holly wasn't going to let her grandmother meddle in her life anymore.

When she looked up to reject the letter, Rex look so earnest that she couldn't find the words to say no.

Instead, Talia stepped in. "I'll take it," she said as she pinched the top of the envelope and pulled it out of Rex's grasp.

Rex opened his mouth to speak, but Holly was ready to get out of the cold, so she turned and headed down the sidewalk, Talia following close behind. She cast a quick smile at Rex as he watched them leave. He nodded and slipped back through the door of his office building.

Thankfully, they had their pick of taxis waiting at the corner. They quickly climbed into the backseat, basking in the warmth that blasted from the vents. Holly told the driver where to go, and he clicked on his blinker to merge into traffic.

Holly settled back on her seat as she allowed her thoughts to still. Talia was not the quiet type and was busy chatting about her family and their plans for the holiday.

Holly found herself relaxing as she listened. It was nice, not having to think. Not having to worry about what she was going to do with Christmas Inn.

Right now, she wasn't going to think about her childhood home or what she'd left behind when she ran away at eighteen.

It was her past, and, after the week-long mandatory stay, it was going to stay in her past. Once and for all.

———

Holly sighed as she felt Tyler's hand on her lower back, guiding her into Le Bouche. Tyler was talking about work, and Holly was happily listening as she plotted ways to tell him that they weren't going to take their annual trip to Honolulu.

Instead they were going to be holed up inside some run-down inn filled with entirely too many bad memories.

It really wasn't the kind of surprise she wanted to lay on him. Tyler wasn't into hotels that didn't have five stars next to their names or luxury spas. The only hope she was holding on to was that once he heard the amount she could get from the sale, he would be more apt to go along.

Pierre, the maître d', was standing at the podium when they approached. He grinned at Tyler and then over at Holly.

"Good evening, Ms. Graham. Mr. Potter," he said in his thick French accent.

Holly smiled at him. "Good evening."

"We are excited you are joining us tonight," he said as he waved for them to follow.

As they moved to follow, they were stopped by the sound of Tyler's phone ringing.

He plopped a kiss on the top of Holly's head as he pulled out his phone. "I've got to grab this. It's the head of the cardiac surgery department." He shot her a sympathetic look. "Order me a scotch?" he asked as he moved toward the far wall.

Holly nodded, then she turned and smiled at Pierre. "I guess we move on."

Pierre motioned toward a nearby table and helped her get situated. Once her chair was pushed forward, he reached over and grabbed her napkin, shook it out, and laid it on her lap.

After ordering a glass of champagne for herself and a scotch for Tyler, Holly settled back in her seat and thought about their upcoming conversation. Tyler wasn't going to be pleased. He reveled in their traveling together.

Where Holly was poor, Tyler was rich. As New York's up-and-coming cardiac surgeon, he had money to spare.

She always felt guilty about her financial situation, so she'd managed to keep it a secret from him. There was this hope, deep down, that she would get herself out of the hole she was in so that if he ever decided to marry her, she wouldn't have this ugly secret hanging over her head.

That was why fulfilling her grandmother's stipulation for the inn was so important. Tyler deserved a great girl ready to leap into a new life with him. Not someone bogged down with regret and pain like she was.

Spending a week at Christmas Inn could change all that.

A hand on her shoulder startled her, and she glanced up to see Tyler's wide smile as he peered down at her. "Hi," he said, leaning down and pressing his lips to hers.

Pushing all other thoughts from her mind, Holly returned the kiss. When Tyler pulled away, he settled into the seat across from her.

"Sorry about that."

Holly shrugged. She was used to it. Tyler was constantly sprinting off to attend to a complicated surgery.

"That was Dr. Jones," Tyler said as he pulled his chair up to the table. Pierre appeared to place the napkin over Tyler's lap and take his order.

Once Tyler was situated, he leaned over and threaded his

fingers together, resting his elbows on the table. "You won't believe what he offered me."

Holly's lips twitched with a smile. "What?"

"He's offered me a position on his Doctors Without Borders excursion."

Holly raised her eyebrows. "Wow. Really? That's so exciting." She sipped at her champagne. "When would you go?"

When Tyler didn't answer right away, she glanced up to see that his lips were pinched and he had a pained expression on his face.

"Tyler?" she asked, fearing what he was going to say.

"I'm sorry, babe. We leave on the fifteenth."

Holly furrowed her brow.

"I know. It changes our holiday plans. But I really want to go. This is my opportunity to work on some complicated issues, get more surgeries under my belt." He leaned forward and smiled. "Which means more money in my pocket."

Holly smiled as she nodded. She knew he thought she was going to be upset by that, but she wasn't. If anything, she was glad. This way, she wasn't the one breaking off their plans.

"Actually, that works well for me. I just found out I have to stay at my grandmother's old inn over the holidays. It's in her will," she said as she nodded to the waiter who set her filet mignon in front of her.

Tyler thanked the waiter, and then they were left alone to eat.

After a few bites, Tyler looked over at her. "Inn? Where?"

Holly swallowed as she finished her bite. "Ivy Springs, Massachusetts."

Tyler winced—just solidifying what she'd thought all along. There was no way Tyler would want to go along with her.

"Yeah, this works out great," he said, raising his glass to clink.

Holly obliged and then brought her glass to her lips.

It felt strange, celebrating that they weren't going to be spending the holiday season together. When she was kid, she'd dreamed of snuggling under the blankets in front of a warm fire with the man she loved.

The fact that he didn't even seem upset that they wouldn't be together…bothered her.

Stupid, childish fantasies.

"We'll get what we need to do done and then be back here, together," Tyler said as he cut through his steak, bringing the bite up to his lips.

"Right," she said, taking another bite.

For the rest of their meal, Tyler looked entirely too much at ease about the whole situation. He didn't look disappointed or upset. If anything, he was giddy with anticipation.

Holly, on the other hand, wasn't sure how she felt. There was something about how he was acting that made her sad. There was a part of her—albeit small—that wanted Tyler to feel sad that they weren't going to be together for the holidays. As much as she didn't want to admit it, spending Christmas without Tyler felt depressing.

The Christmas holiday already held so many bad memories, she didn't want this to be one of them.

But, from the sinking feeling in her stomach, that was going to be the case. Whether she wanted it or not.

What a holly, jolly Christmas.

HOLLY

To Whom It May Concern:

  I am writing to inform you of my upcoming trip to Christmas Inn.

As you might know, I am the new owner. I have no intention of keeping the inn, but due to a stipulation in Hope Graham's will, I'll be spending Christmas there.

I would appreciate your cooperation in removing all Christmas decorations from the house and from my room specifically.

I understand the draw to Christmas Inn is the merriment of this time of year, but the inn will be sold at the end of my stay, and I'm not interested in spending time surrounded by the obscene amount of decorations my grandmother always put out.

I will also be assessing the land. If you could prep it for me to do so, I would appreciate it.

Thank you for your attention on this matter, and I look forward to seeing you on December 20th. My flight gets in at 3 p.m. Please have someone pick me up at that time.

Ms. Graham

. . .

Holly stood in her small bedroom, staring at the suitcase she had laid out in front of her. Talia was perched on the end of the bed, scrolling through her phone with a smile on her face.

Tomorrow, Holly would be on a plane heading to Ivy Springs. To say she was regretting this trip would be putting it mildly.

Tyler had already left for Doctors Without Borders with a kiss and a wave. He wasn't going to be back for at least three months.

Holly fiddled with the necklace he had given her as she blew out her breath. She wished he'd decided to stay, but she knew how much his career meant to him, and she didn't want to be the one to drag him down.

Plus, Christmas Inn was her problem to bear. She was going to take this time to say goodbye to her grandmother and leave behind all the hurt that had surrounded their relationship.

Living without her parents had always caused a hollow ache to rise up in her chest. Her father had never been in her life. And, growing up, she'd always believed that she'd been the reason her mother left.

It wasn't until she was eighteen that she learned it was her grandmother who had driven her mother from the house. And told her to never come back. Her grandmother was the reason Holly had been abandoned.

And when the truth came to life, Holly left. She couldn't imagine living in a house with someone who would lie to her like that. Someone who would allow her to think she was responsible for her mother's sudden departure from her life.

That wasn't in harmony with the Christmas cheer her grandmother peddled at the inn. And it wasn't something a grandmother did to her granddaughter.

Whatever Holly's mother had done, she hadn't deserved to get thrown from the house.

"Oh no." Talia's voice cut through Holly's reverie.

Holly blinked a few times as she glanced over at her best friend. "What?" she asked as she grabbed a black oversized hoodie and slipped it over her head. She wrapped her arms around her chest, enjoying the soft, warm fabric that enveloped her.

"You're getting that dazed look again," Talia said as she set her phone down on the bed. She flipped to her back and stared up at the ceiling.

Holly laughed as she pulled her suitcase off the bed so that she could join Talia. She threaded her fingers together and rested them on her stomach.

"Are you sure you don't want me to come with you?" Talia asked, tipping her head in Holly's direction.

Holly blinked a few times but then shook her head. "No. I'll be fine. It'll only be a little over a week. Once I've fulfilled Hope's wish, I'll be back and ready to move on."

Talia nodded as she moved to stare back up at the ceiling. "It might be fun," she offered. She sounded like she was trying to convince a toddler that getting poked by a needle would be fun.

Holly laughed. "I'm not sure I would use the word *fun*, but I'm sure I'll survive."

Talia grew quiet. "What is Christmas Inn like? I mean, is it Christmasy all year long?"

Holly stared up at the ceiling. "Yes and no. During the year, it's got some Christmas decorations, but not like during the holiday season. My grandmother goes all out right after Halloween. Decorations. Lights. The whole shebang." Realizing what she just said, she quickly corrected herself. "Used to. She used to do that..."

Holly's voice trailed off. She pinched her lips as a dull ache rose inside of her. That was not a trip down memory lane that she wanted to take.

Talia reached over and patted Holly's hand. "Alrighty, let's get you packed," she said as she pulled herself into a sitting position.

Holly stayed on the bed a few seconds longer before she too sat up and stretched out her arms. "I guess it's now or never." She stood and returned her suitcase to its original place.

With Talia's help, packing went much faster than if Holly had been alone, drowning her sorrow in Irish coffee while listening to Sarah McLachlan. There was always a part of her that connected to the soulful way she sang, "*Angel.*"

So the fact that Talia was here, keeping her from going down that road, meant everything was packed up and her suitcase was zipped shut before Holly could even finish her coffee.

Talia got a phone call and leaned in to kiss Holly on the cheek and tell her to have a great trip. Holly tried not to scoff as she showed Talia out. As soon as she got to the hallway, Talia had her phone pressed to her cheek and was laughing along with her mom.

Holly leaned on her doorjamb as she folded her arms and watched Talia board the elevator, the doors sliding shut behind her.

Now, very much alone, Holly walked back into her apartment and shut the door. She grabbed a doughnut from the box that Tyler had left her and padded into the living room, where she cuddled up in her pile of blankets. Their soft texture tickled her skin and helped her calm down.

She grabbed the remote and flipped the TV on. The sound of the Home Shopping Network filled the silence. She settled back on the couch and devoured the doughnut faster than she cared to admit. Once it was gone, she licked the glaze from her fingertips and snuggled deep into the blankets.

Her apartment was small and furnished with pieces she'd found in the lobby of her building. It wasn't anything magical, but it was a place she could call home. And thankfully, Tyler never seemed interested in coming to her place—she quickly side-stepped his questions when he asked.

Her sewing machine was set up in the corner. Racks of unfinished projects lined the room, and scraps of fabric littered the floor.

She'd been having such a hard time creating lately. It was cold and dreary in New York. And the constant holiday merriment was enough to make her want to curl up in bed and never come out.

Sighing, she shifted her gaze to her bulletin board, finding the letter that Rex had given her. The one her grandmother had written.

Pain squeezed her chest, so she dropped her gaze and focused back on the TV. She really didn't want to know what her grandmother had written. In fact, all she wanted to do was rip the letter up and throw it away.

There couldn't be anything on that piece of paper that she wanted to know. Her grandmother had said everything ten years ago. What other information could she possibly give?

But, no matter how hard Holly tried to ignore that little white envelope, she couldn't. Sighing, she pulled off her blankets and stood. She made her way over to the board and pulled the tack from the top corner, allowing the envelope to fall into her open hand.

She might as well take it with her. Maybe there was something in there about the sale of the property that she might need to know.

Here she was, assuming that her grandmother's letter was an attempt to reach out to her to make amends, when it could just as easily contain some facts or information about the inn. And what if she needed whatever was in it when she signed the papers?

Holly clutched the envelope in her hand as she walked back over to the couch and clicked off the TV. Then she yawned and made her way to her bedroom, where she tucked the envelope into her suitcase.

It didn't take long to wash her face and brush her teeth. She sighed as she climbed into bed and pulled the covers up to her neck, allowing her body to sink into the mattress.

A sense of relief rushed over her as she thought about her trip. She only needed to survive one week at the inn.

One week for her to fulfill the stipulation and move on with her life. Her grandmother and Christmas Inn would soon be but a distant memory. One she could tuck away in the back of her mind and never revisit.

Her body felt heavy as she closed her eyes and allowed sleep to overtake her.

3

STEPHEN

"**D**am—dang it," Stephen said, catching himself before he cursed. He was in the process of pulling out the salt from the back of his truck and had managed to bang his leg on the trailer extension of the carriage he had parked in the garage to keep it out of the snow.

Isaac popped up from behind the salt with his finger pressed to his lips. "Uncle Steppen said a naughty word."

Stephen pursed his lips as he shot his nephew a guilty look. "I know, I'm sorry. I won't do it again."

Isaac shrugged, obviously having moved on from Stephen's blunder, and was busy trying to wedge his body between the bags of salt and the truck. He pressed his tiny six-year-old shoulder into the salt and pushed. Stephen laughed as Isaac grunted. The bag hadn't moved an inch.

"You helping, buddy?" Stephen asked as he grabbed another bag and hoisted it up onto his shoulder, this time steering clear of the carriage.

Isaac grunted again before Stephen heard him collapse in the bed of the truck. "These are heavy," the little boy declared.

Stephen grabbed another bag and nodded. "Well, they are when they weigh as much as you do."

Isaac climbed to the top of the stack and peered down at Stephen. "Am I going to be as big as you someday?"

Stephen shrugged. "Probably. You know, your mom and I are siblings. We share the same genes."

Isaac wrinkled his nose. "I don't want to wear girl pants."

Stephen paused as Isaac's words rolled around in his mind. Then a chuckle escaped when he realized what Isaac was saying.

"Genes are the code that your body uses to determine if your hair is brown or blond. Not 'jeans' like what you wear." He hoisted another bag on his shoulder.

From the confused look on Isaac's face, he realized there was no way his nephew was going to understand, so he decided to keep things simple.

"Yes, you will grow to be as big as I am," he said as he rested the last bag on the pile he'd made at the far end of the garage. He returned to the truck to hoist his nephew out.

He flung Isaac over his shoulder and spun him around a few times. Isaac let out a giggle as he flung his arms out.

"I'm flying!" he squealed.

Stephen let go of the stress that seemed to be suffocating him and laughed as well.

To say he was struggling under a mountain of responsibility would be an understatement.

Christmas Inn was in trouble. Hope was gone, and in a matter of minutes, he was going to have to climb back into his truck and pick up the one girl he'd never forgotten but who had no problem forgetting him.

Holly.

He cleared his throat as he lowered Isaac to the ground.

There was no reason to dwell on what he knew was coming. He was going to hold out hope that Holly wasn't really going to sell the inn. There was a chance that she would arrive, remember the memories they shared here, and change her mind.

He just needed to ignore the sinking feeling inside of his stomach. He was going to be able to keep running Christmas Inn while taking care of his sister and nephew. He was going to. He had no other option.

The alarm on his phone sounded, and he slipped out his phone to silence it. It was time to leave. Time to get Holly.

Christmas Inn got an email the week before from *"Ms. Graham" letting them know she was coming.* Stephen was choosing to ignore the fact that she still wasn't married. He couldn't allow thoughts like that to roll around in his mind. She was off limits. Period.

She'd addressed it, "to whom this may concern," like she was some pretentious socialite. Which was comical as Stephen thought back to fond memories of Holly in braces and pigtails. So when Stephen had read her letter, he'd laughed out loud and hard.

Apparently, she knew nothing about the inn or that it was his job to run it. She wanted them to take down the Christmas decorations? Was she serious?

Christmas was literally in the inn's name. Plus, he was booked solid for the month. There was no way he was going to take down the decorations.

Ms. Hoity-toity was in for a rude awakening when she got here. Stephen had half a mind to stuff her room full of decorations just to make a point. But he hadn't. Blossom had told him to rise above, which he was trying to do—until he'd had seven Christmas trees delivered, and the empty room had just seemed like the perfect place.

What Blossom didn't know wouldn't kill her.

He was also trying not to get too giddy about surprising Holly when he showed up at the airport to pick her up. Especially since she clearly had no idea that he was still here.

The shock on her face would be his very own Christmas present.

At the end of her letter, Holly talked about assessing the property, which was a passive way of saying she was going to prep it for sale. Stephen wasn't stupid. He knew that in an up-and-coming town like Ivy Springs, the thirty-acre property the inn sat on was in high demand.

A development company could build numerous houses on that much land. They'd fill in the backyard pond and sell each lot for top dollar. Holly had inherited a multimillion dollar piece of land.

Except, it wasn't just a piece of land. Christmas Inn was iconic. Couples came here every year to make new memories or celebrate old ones.

The fact that Holly saw Christmas Inn as just an item to sell off...well, it made Stephen's blood boil.

Isaac's small face popped up in front of Stephen. His nephew was studying him.

"Are you mad?" Isaac asked.

"Nope." He hoisted Isaac up onto his shoulder again and made his way out through the garage door and across the covered walkway to the porch. When he got to the kitchen door, he swung it open and kicked the snow off his boots as he set Isaac down.

"Hey, bud, I'm running to the airport to pick someone up. Can you hold down the fort for me?" Just then, Mrs. Brondy walked in with her glasses perched on her nose and an apron tied around her waist. Flour dusted her face as she peered at them.

"Heading out now?" she asked as she brushed off her hands.

"Yeah. I have to go pick up the new boss."

Mrs. Brondy's expression turned sad with a hint of nostalgia. She had been at Christmas Inn for as long as Stephen could remember. Her food was legendary. Even the town's residents came to eat at the small dining room of Christmas Inn.

She had been best friends with Hope and knew Holly well. She'd had a front seat to the pain both experienced when the truth about Holly's mother had come to light. And to have Holly leave like she did, well it broke a lot of hearts.

Truth was, Holly had left a lot of people. And it still hurt—even if Stephen didn't want to admit it. He hated seeing that hurt in the eyes of people he cared about.

They deserved better than what Holly Graham had given them. They were family, and you never turn your back on family. That was the motto Stephen lived by.

He reached out and kissed Mrs. Brondy on the cheek as he passed. "I'm going to say a quick goodbye to Blossom and then head out," he called over his shoulder as he made his way into the dining room.

As he walked out, he heard Mrs. Brondy ask if Isaac would help her bake some cookies, to which the little boy quite loudly agreed.

He couldn't fight the smile that emerged as he slipped past the abandoned reception desk. He found his sister in her wheelchair, sitting in front of the large bay window across from the desk.

She had a forlorn look on her face as she stared out at the setting sun. Stephen could tell that she was deep in thought, and he almost left her alone but then decided against it.

"Hey, sis," he said as he settled down on the window seat he'd built three years ago. It was as sturdy as the day he'd built it.

Her gaze flickered over to him, and her lips tipped up into a smile. "Hey," she said as she adjusted the blanket over her lap.

Four years ago, she was in an accident. It had left both legs weakened. It took some convincing, but with Hope's approval, Stephen had been able to persuade Blossom to bring Isaac to Christmas Inn to live.

And they'd stayed. Christmas Inn was as much their home as it was his.

"I've got to run to the airport to grab the new boss," he said with a hint of sarcasm. Blossom picked up on it and gave him a very unamused look.

"Isaac?" she asked as she turned to glance behind her.

"With Mrs. Brondy. They're making cookies," Stephen said as he stood and shrugged.

Blossom's jaw dropped. "Before dinner? Doesn't she know it will ruin his appetite? It's already such a pain to get him to eat." She started rolling toward the kitchen door.

"Guests?" Stephen called after her.

Blossom waved him away as she disappeared. Stephen chuckled as he heard the voices of Blossom and Mrs. Brondy and then the very loud and disappointed whine of Isaac.

Stephen checked the guest log just to make sure they had no new arrivals that evening, and then he grabbed his jacket and slipped his keys into his pocket.

After grabbing an apple from the counter, he waved to the three in the kitchen and then headed out to the garage. He climbed into his truck and started the engine.

Christmas music blared from the speakers—thanks to Isaac's insistence. Taking a bite of the apple, Stephen held it between his teeth as he reached over and turned the music down.

Then he backed out of the driveway and pulled out onto the main road. Once he was settled into his seat, he pulled the apple away and chewed thoughtfully as he allowed his mind to wander.

Every so often, he tapped his fingers on the steering wheel in time with the music.

He'd known this day would come eventually. The day that Holly returned. And he'd been prepared—or so he'd thought.

But now his stomach was in knots and, with a two-hour drive to go, he wasn't sure he was ready for anything anymore.

What was she going to do? How much had she changed?

Hope had been cremated at her wish two months ago. There had been no funeral service. The ashes had been sent to Holly and that was it.

The Christmas Inn held a memorial in her honor, but Holly didn't come. Stephen wasn't sure what he thought of that. In fact, he tried to push that detail from his mind. It wasn't going to do anyone any good to dwell on the past.

He was thankful for the two-hour drive to the airport. It gave him time to think. And by the time he pulled into the parking garage, he felt as if he could breathe again. Perhaps he was going to be able to face this next week with Holly coming home.

Hope always seemed to have a plan. If bringing Holly home for one more Christmas was part of that, then he would go along with it. Even from the grave, that woman was controlling everything that happened at Christmas Inn.

The thought of Hope smiling down on them while they carried out her plan made him chuckle as he undid his seat belt and swung open his door. He jumped from the truck and tightened his jacket around himself as he turned and slammed the door behind him.

He shoved both hands into his jacket pockets and made his way across the parking garage. Once inside the terminal, he found a monitor and located Holly's flight.

Baggage claim carousel number seven.

He nodded at a few people who'd gathered around him as he passed by and made his way over to the large conveyor that had been activated and was spitting out luggage.

"Stephen?"

Her voice stopped him dead in his tracks. His shoulders tightened as he kept his gaze fixed in front of him.

He should have known he would recognize Holly's voice. It wasn't like it didn't replay in his mind every so often. There were times when memories of her haunted his dreams. Especially when he would drive by the secret spots they had run away to as kids. Or when he would pass by her photo on the inn's wall.

All of it reminded him of the woman he once loved.

Now, hearing her voice, chills erupted across his skin. His breath caught in his throat. He needed to prepare himself to turn around. To face her.

The real her.

"What are you doing here?" she asked.

Realizing that he looked like an idiot, having Holly talk to his back, he slowly turned around. He brought his gaze up to see her bright blue eyes. She looked older and—if he was brave enough to admit it—as beautiful as ever. Age had only enhanced the splash of freckles across her nose, and the creaminess of her skin was accented by her dark brown and very tamed hair. No more frizz and spastic curls. Instead, her hair glistened in the florescent lighting.

She raised her eyebrows as she leaned toward him.

Embarrassed that he was staring, Stephen pushed his hands through his hair and glanced around, noting the suitcase that was trailing behind her.

"Are you ready?" he asked, which was a ridiculous question. Of course she was ready. She was standing in front of him with her suitcase. What else would she be waiting for?

Her gaze followed his down to her suitcase and then back up to him. "Yes," she said.

He nodded, and then, desperate for something to do, he moved to take her suitcase. His fingers brushed hers and a wave of heat rushed up his arm.

He jerked his hand back just as she uncurled her fingers, releasing the handle.

The suitcase landed on the floor with a thump.

Embarrassment coursed through Stephen as he avoided her gaze and bent down to lift it up. "Sorry," he muttered, nodding toward the sliding doors. "I'm out this way."

From the corner of his eye, he saw Holly glance toward the doors and then follow after him. She quickened her pace to keep up.

"So, you're still at Christmas Inn?" she asked, pulling on her gloves. The cold air blasted around them as they stepped out of the airport and into the parking garage.

"Yes." Stephen welcomed the cool air. It helped calm his frazzled nerves. He unlocked the truck's doors and made his way to the passenger side to open the door for her.

Then he stood there, like an idiot, as he waited for Holly to climb inside.

She furrowed her brow a bit but then grabbed onto the handle and lifted herself into the seat.

Stephen tried not to notice the curves of her body as she moved. She was no longer the tall, skinny girl he remembered. She was a woman now. Clearing his throat, he set her suitcase in the bed of the truck and then he jogged over to the driver's door.

Before he opened it, he took a deep breath.

He could do this. He could survive this Christmas with Holly at the inn. He couldn't allow this resurfacing of emotions to distract him from his goal—convincing Holly not to sell. Keeping the inn was all that mattered.

Now, if he could only convince his heart, he would be golden.

4

HOLLY

Holly wasn't sure who she expected to find when she exited the plane and collected her luggage. Maybe some young kid from Ivy Springs who'd picked up a shift at the inn. Or...who knows.

What she didn't expect was to come face to face with Stephen Jones.

She had to admit, when she first saw him standing there with his wind-blown hair, chiseled jaw, and bright green eyes, her heart stopped for a minute.

Time had been kind to him. He was taller, more built, and much more handsome than she wanted to acknowledge. When he stared into her eyes, it was like she was transported to the past. Back to a time when things were simpler. When she trusted people. When she allowed herself to love.

Blinking a few times, Holly fiddled with her hair as she stared out the truck's window at the scenery that passed by. Everything was covered with snow. The sun had set, and the lights of passing cars mixed with the moon, causing the snow to glisten and shine. If she wasn't heading back to the place she'd spent her whole adult life avoiding, she might have felt at peace.

An ache she'd pushed way down inside of her resurfaced, and she paused as she allowed it to settle in around her. Why couldn't her life be simpler? Why did things have to be so hard?

Not wanting to lose her mind by obsessing over things she couldn't change, Holly folded her arms across her chest and snuck a peek at Stephen.

He was resting his elbow on the central console while his other wrist was draped over the steering wheel. His jaw was set, and for a moment, Holly wondered why.

And then she felt stupid. She knew why he was uncomfortable. They had parted on less than favorable terms. That night had been horrible for everyone involved. The things she'd said couldn't be taken back, so why even try?

Stephen was her past. Tyler was her future.

"How was your flight?" Stephen asked.

Glancing over, she saw that his gaze remained focused on the road. She wondered for a moment if he'd even spoken then he flicked his gaze over to her.

"Uneventful," she replied as she shifted in her seat.

Why was she so uncomfortable? She was a full-grown woman, and she'd moved on a long time ago. Since settling down in New York, there hadn't been many times when she even thought about Stephen.

Sure, on occasion, when she'd had a little too much to drink, memories of him managed to make their way back into her mind, but that was it.

Sitting here, fully sober, she should be able to have a normal conversation with him. Something beyond inane pleasantries.

She hated how formal everything felt.

"So you couldn't be bothered to tell me it would be you picking me up?" As the words tumbled from her lips, she winced. She hadn't meant for it to come out so accusatory. She'd need to watch that.

Stephen scoffed as he changed his hands and shifted his

weight. "I wouldn't have to tell you if you actually visited once in a while." The bite in his tone matched her own, but she understood it.

If anything, she welcomed it. It made him feel more human and her less like a witch.

But, talking about the past and why she left wasn't what she wanted to do on this trip. Instead of answering him, she just folded her arms tighter and sighed.

"What do you do at Christmas Inn?" she asked as she peeked over at him. She wanted to know how much he was going to be around. Since part of the proceeds from the sale of the inn were supposed to go to him, she'd suspected he was still involved.

"I work there," he grumbled. "I sort of run the place."

Stephen shifted the wheel to the right and pulled off the highway and into a small gas station. He threw the truck into park and opened his door, blasting her with chilly air.

She sucked in her breath, determined to say something in response, but he slammed his door before she could get a syllable out. He moved to the side of the truck and she could hear scraping as he began to fill the tank.

Shaking her head, she sighed as she dropped her hands into her lap and fiddled with her fingernails.

Their conversation wasn't making her feel any better. If anything, she felt more frustrated. Stephen working for the inn was one thing, but running it?

She was going to have to see him far more than she liked, and that was going to make this trip even harder.

Taking in a deep breath, she glanced outside. Stephen had finished pumping gas and was walking by the windshield with his head tipped down and his hands shoved into his jacket pockets.

He quickened his pace as he crossed the parking lot and pulled open the convenience store's door. Once he disappeared inside, Holly released the breath that she didn't realize she'd been holding.

With him gone, she felt as if she could breathe a little easier. Reaching into her purse, she pulled out her phone and swiped it on. She located Talia's number.

Holly: So, interesting turn of events. Stephen picked me up.

She pressed send and waited for a response. Which, in true Talia fashion, came a few seconds later.

Talia: Who's Stephen?

Holly blew out her breath. She knew she'd mentioned Stephen to Talia at least once. Right?

Holly: Stephen. The guy I grew up with and sorta kinda dated

She sent it off and waited, watching the dots that faded in and out as Talia typed on the other end.

Talia: Never heard of him. Is this good or bad?

Holly sighed as her gaze flicked over to the convenience store. She could see Stephen standing near the cash register, pulling out his wallet. She studied him, trying to assess the feelings that were swirling around inside her.

Good? Bad? She wasn't sure. She didn't know what she was supposed to think about any of this. Coming back to Ivy Springs hadn't been in her plans.

Holly: It's nothing. Just…interesting.

She finished with a shrugging emoji.

There was a pause and then Talia responded.

Talia: I think it's something. Quick, send me a pic. I want to see what this guy looks like.

Heat permeated Holly's cheeks as she glanced up to see Stephen walking toward her. There was no way she wanted to snap a photo of him. And she most definitely didn't want to send it to Talia.

Holly knew a good-looking guy when she saw one, and Stephen was definitely good-looking. Just off his build, she knew he was hiding some serious muscles under that shirt and jacket he had on.

And then, just as luck would have it, Stephen raised his gaze and met Holly's. Like a deer in headlights, it took a moment before Holly registered what was happening.

Embarrassment coursed through her as she dropped her gaze. She sent Talia an eye rolling emoji and shoved her phone back into her purse. She cursed her friend for distracting her. Now Stephen knew that she'd been watching him.

The driver's door opened, and Stephen climbed into the car. He handed over a cup of coffee.

"Coffee with cream and one sugar," he said as she took it from him.

For a moment, she paused. "You remembered?"

Stephen glanced over at her as he set his cup into the holder next to him and shoved the keys into the ignition. The engine roared to life as he cast a smile her direction.

It was soft and sweet and caused her toes to tingle. Or maybe that was from the negative temperature outside.

Yeah, she was going to go with that.

"Of course. It's my job to remember things like this," he said as he shifted the car into drive and pressed on the gas.

Not sure what to say, Holly wrapped her hands around the cup, reveling in its warmth. She sipped it only to have the scalding liquid burn her tongue. While she waited for it to cool, she rested her the cup in her lap and huddled over it, hoping it would provide her with the warmth she was lacking.

Stephen adjusted the heat on the dash. She glanced over at him, and he smiled at her.

"I run warm," he said and then wrinkled his nose. "I'm sorry. That came out wrong." He cleared his throat as he shifted in his seat again. "You looked cold," he said.

Holly just nodded. "Thanks."

She felt bad that he was being so nice. She was here to shut the inn down, and it seemed that doing so would most definitely affect him. She didn't want him to go out of his way to be nice to her.

She was determined to sell and move on with her life. He had to know that.

"The appraiser is coming two days after Christmas. Do you think we'll have everything ready in time?" she asked as she raised her cup to her lips and took a sip.

When Stephen didn't respond, she glanced over at him. He was gripping the steering wheel so hard his knuckles were white. His jaw was set, and she could tell she'd struck a nerve.

"I really don't want to think about that until after Christmas," he said in a short and curt tone. He reached over and lifted his cup to his lips.

"Stephen, I realize—"

"No. You don't. You don't realize anything." His abrupt response caused her to pull back.

She understood he was upset, but he didn't have to treat her that way. The inn had been her home. She knew what it meant to a lot of people. At some point, though, a person had to be sensible. And that was what she was doing. Being sensible.

"I know you hate me," she said as she glanced down at her cup. She shut her eyes as she waited for his response.

"I don't hate you. No one does," he finally said, cutting through the deafening silence. She moved to take a breath, but then he added, "But if you ruin this Christmas with your talk of selling, I will hate you." He took another sip of his coffee and returned it to the cup holder.

Then he leaned forward and flicked on the radio.

"I saw Mommy Kissing Santa Claus" blared from the speakers, causing Holly to wince. She wanted to say something but decided against it.

From the way Stephen was hunched forward, resting his weight on his elbow, she knew that he was trying to protect himself. She'd seen him like that many times in the past.

It was strange, facing Stephen like this. It was amazing how quickly the memories came flooding back to her. All it took was one look, one conversation, and everything she'd ever tried to forget was brought to the surface.

It scared her.

She had half a mind to demand that Stephen turn around and drive her back to the airport. Spending the holidays wrapped up in bitter memories didn't seem like the vacation Rex or Tyler had made it out to be.

She was going to have to deal with the ghosts of her past whether she wanted to or not.

Closing her eyes, she focused her mind on the reason she was here. Sometimes, to move on from the past, one had to face it first. She was here for closure on her relationship with her grandmother and the inn. She couldn't allow her fear to distract her.

With a plan set in her mind, she was confident that she would be able to hold things together enough to make it through the week.

But, when Stephen turned down the familiar driveway that lead up to the inn, her heart began to hammer in her chest. She took in a few deep breaths and forced a smile to her lips.

I can do this. I can do this, she chanted in her mind.

Stephen pulled into the garage off to the side of the inn. It was built in front of the horse stables that she could see as he neared. She'd loved riding horses as a kid. There was something magical about spending time out in nature. To see the world from the back of the majestic animals.

She was going to have to go for a ride as soon as she was settled.

Once Stephen had pulled in far enough, he pushed the truck into park. "I'll get your bags," he said as he opened his door and jumped down.

Holly sat there for a moment as thoughts rolled around in her mind. She hated the way she'd ended her conversation with Stephen. After all, he deserved better than she had given him.

Truth was, when she thought back on her actions, she couldn't help but acknowledge that her leaving had hurt people—herself included. Her grandmother should have never done what she did.

Throwing Holly's mother from the inn and demanding that she never return wasn't a choice she should have made. Holly hadn't been given the choice of whether or not to have her mother in her life; her grandmother had made that decision for her.

And it hurt. Just as deeply as it had ten years ago.

Clearing her throat, Holly pushed those feelings of betrayal down deep. She needed to let them go and focus.

She reached her fingers out and grabbed the door handle. She pushed the door with her shoulder, and it swung open. Stephen had already disappeared through the garage door with her suitcase in hand.

Now alone, she let out the breath she'd been holding as she glanced around. Boxes lined the walls. Boxes that held all of her grandmother's Christmas decorations. Everything she caught a glimpse of caused a wave of memories to wash over her.

Shouldering her purse, she ducked her head and made her way through the garage door, out across the covered patio, and over to the kitchen door. She closed her eyes for a moment to mentally prepare herself.

She reached out and grabbed the door handle. She might as well get this over with.

5

STEPHEN

The dining room was full of guests—mostly residents of Ivy Springs who'd booked a stay after Hope passed. Holly's suitcase bumped against his leg as he stepped out of the kitchen. Warmth surrounded him, and the smell of chicken potpie filled his nose.

The soft sound of instrumental Christmas music carried through the room. Muffled conversations were broken up by the sound of silverware clinking against plates.

Stephen felt his stress lessen as he set down Holly's luggage and looked around. Even though the room held sparse Christmas decorations—the ones that stayed up all year round— no one really seemed bothered by it. Every time he apologized to a guest for the lack of Christmas cheer, they just shook their head, patted his arm, and told him not to worry about it. They understood. In a small town, everyone came together to help others out. And that was what this Christmas was about, helping out after Hope passed.

Stephen was grateful for their forgiveness, but he didn't want to let Hope down by doing the job she'd left to him anything less than perfectly. He knew this couldn't last forever, the entire town staying at Christmas Inn. He needed to restore this place to its former glory.

Hope's memory deserved so much more than what he was giving.

The swinging kitchen door smacked into him. He stepped out of the way and glanced over his shoulder to see the wide eyes of Holly. Her skin was pink, and her hair was tousled. She pulled her coat closer as she glanced around the room.

When her gaze landed on Stephen, she gave him a quick nod.

Feeling like an idiot for how he'd acted on the drive, he opened his mouth to apologize, only to be drowned out by Mrs. Brondy yelling from the other end of the dining room.

"Holly, you're here! You came!" Her hands were clasped together as she weaved her way through the tables. Holly looked alarmed, but if Mrs. Brondy noticed, it didn't dissuade her. She reached out and pulled Holly into a hug.

"We've missed you around here," Mrs. Brondy said, her voice muffled by Holly's jacket.

Holly patted Mrs. Brondy's back in a slow, methodical manner.

Stephen folded his arms across his chest, completely ready to be entertained. Holly had been anything but pleasant to him, and he was interested to see if the woman he once knew was still in there, or if Holly was just as pretentious as he feared she'd become.

From where he stood, it was clear she'd changed. And not in a good way.

"Thank you, Mrs. Brondy," Holly said when she was finally released from the hug. Stephen studied her as she smiled. There was definitely hurt in her expression, but her smile was genuine.

And familiar.

A hollow ache rose inside of Stephen as he reached down to grab the suitcase next to him. This wasn't the time or place to slip into memories of Holly.

She'd made her choice a long time ago. She'd walked away from this place, from him. And it was up to him to make sure his feelings for her stayed buried.

Nothing good could come from loving Holly. She was intent on selling Christmas Inn and that was that. The woman who was willing to give up on the magic that this place held wasn't the Holly he knew anymore.

"Uncle Steppen!"

Stephen glanced around and saw Isaac standing on his chair at the table in the far corner. He was bouncing up and down, waving his hands. Blossom was next to him, frantically grabbing at him and commanding that he sit down.

But Isaac wasn't interested in listening. He had gotten very good as moving just far enough of his mom's reach so that he could continue doing whatever he wanted.

Ready to put to bed those pesky feelings that had crept up inside of him since Holly climbed into the cab of his truck, he moved over to stand behind Isaac's chair. In true Isaac fashion, the boy wrapped his arms around Stephen and scaled him like a monkey.

To keep Isaac from dropping to the floor, Stephen hoisted him up onto his shoulders. Isaac giggled.

"You spoil him, you know," Blossom said. She'd settled back in her wheelchair and folded her arms.

Stephen glanced over at his sister and gave her a wink. "Someone has to do it."

Blossom's lips twitched as she attempted to keep a straight face. Isaac wrapped his little hands under Stephen's chin and dipped down so his lips were pressed to Stephen's ear.

"Who's that?" Isaac asked in a whisper, sticking out his pudgy finger.

Stephen followed his gesture. He was pointing at Holly, who was still talking to Mrs. Brondy. She was clutching the strap of her purse as if she were hanging onto it for dear life.

Her expression was pained, and it was evident that she was pushing through whatever reservations she had about being here.

It was so strange, her resistance to Christmas Inn. Anyone who came here instantly fell in love with the place. Well, maybe not right then. With the sparse decorations, even Stephen was having a hard time remembering that it was Christmas.

But that was all going to change. Starting tomorrow, he was going to hit the ground running. He didn't care what Holly said about Christmas cheer. If this was the last Christmas he was going to spend at the inn he'd grown up loving, he was going to make it one to remember.

Reaching up, he grabbed onto Isaac's arm and slid the little boy down from his shoulders. Then he set him back onto the chair, butt down this time, and crouched down next to his nephew.

Isaac glanced up at him with his wide brown eyes.

"Remember that movie we watched last weekend? The one with the Grinch, whose heart needed to grow?" Stephen studied his nephew until he saw a spark of recognition.

Isaac began to nod enthusiastically.

Stephen smiled as he tousled Isaac's hair. "Well, that lady over there, she's the Grinch's sister—"

"Stephen," Blossom hissed.

His sister's eyes were wide and her lips pinched together. He furrowed his brow. "What?"

"You cannot tell Isaac that. What's he going to say to her?" Blossom's cheeks were red as she studied him.

Stephen shrugged. "Hey, if it's true, it's true." There was a slight tug on his heart that told him it wasn't the whole truth. Holly had a good reason to be upset with her grandmother, to want to sell this place. But he wasn't going to focus on that.

In the end, the inn would be sold, and he would be left to find a new home for Blossom, Isaac, and himself. Nothing would be quite as perfect as this place.

But he wasn't going to let it go without a fight. Even if that meant his nephew might call Holly a grinch.

Blossom just shook her head as she sipped the soup from her spoon.

Thankful that Blossom wasn't going to push him further about this, he turned his attention over to Isaac, who was still staring at him with wide eyes and parted lips.

At least he had his six-year-old nephew on his side. He cleared his throat and focused back on what he was saying.

"It's our job this Christmas to help her heart grow," he said, tipping his head toward Holly.

Isaac snuck a peek at Holly and then glanced back at Stephen. "Okay," he whispered and then giggled. As if he were thrilled with their plan.

"I'm ready to see my room now," Holly's voice sounded from above them.

Stephen took a moment to wink at Isaac—who giggled even more—and then straightened.

"Welcome home, Holly," Blossom said as she smiled over at her.

Holly's eyes widened as she studied Stephen's sister. "Blossom? H-hey, I didn't know you were in town," she said as she bent down to give Blossom a hug.

"Yeah, moved here a few years ago. Right after the accident," Blossom said matter-of-factly, and Stephen held his breath, wondering what Holly was going to say.

He peeked over at her. Her lips were pinched together, and there was an air of awkwardness that was making him itch. If Holly had ever bothered to come home, she would have known about Blossom. She would have been there for him while they worked through the accident and rehabilitation.

But Holly hadn't been there. And he'd been alone.

Not wanting to share with Holly a piece of his life that she'd given up the right to take part in years ago, he grabbed her suitcase's handle and extended his arm. "This way." He was desperate to get her out of the dining room and upstairs, where she would be out of his hair—at least for now.

Holly glanced over at him and nodded. "Right. Thanks." She sighed and glanced over at Blossom and Isaac. "Well, it was good to see you again."

Blossom nodded and then turned her attention to Isaac, who was flinging noodles across the room with his spoon.

Stephen didn't even wait to see if Holly followed after him. He turned and made his way over to the central staircase, where he began to climb the stairs two by two.

"We were booked solid, but we had a cancellation. That's why you're not staying in the stalls," he added under his breath as he grabbed out his key ring and unlocked the door to the suite at the end of the hall.

Holly laughed—it sounded strained and unfamiliar—but when he gave her a serious look, her laughter died.

He hadn't been joking. Sure it was a juvenile move, but he was hurting. The inn was his. What did Holly care when she was hell-bent on selling it? In turning the land into cookie-cutter houses?

"Oh," she said as she walked past him. But she paused when she got into the room.

As a joke, Stephen had decided to store all the Christmas trees in her room. After all, he hadn't expected it to be occupied once the couple who was going to stay there canceled.

Plus, it seemed Holly could use a little holiday cheer in her life.

So, he'd decided to keep them there, in all their pine-smelling glory, until they got around to bringing them downstairs for decorating.

"I thought I asked not to have any Christmas decorations in my room," she said, holding up her finger as she turned back to him.

Stephen leaned against the doorframe and nodded. "Right. I

got that *e-mail*. 'To whom it may concern,' " he said with air quotes.

Holly pinched her lips together. "I didn't know you were still here."

Stephen snorted. "Yeah. I figured."

She sighed as she threw up her arms. "So, how long am I going to be Snow White in the woods?"

Stephen straightened as he reached for the door handle and began pulling the door closed. "When do you plan on selling?" he asked.

She gave him an annoyed look. "You know how long I'm—"

"Until then," he said, shutting the door and cutting off her words.

He stood in the hallway with his back pressed against the dark oak door. He took in a deep breath, feeling slightly better about his situation. Holly had a major anti-Christmas stick up her butt. That woman in there wasn't the girl he'd grown up with. She wasn't the girl he'd fallen in love with. She was the Grinch.

This Christmas, he was determined to find that stick and remove it. It was his only chance to save not only the holiday season, but the inn itself.

He had a job to do and he was going to do it. Holly Graham was no match for him. He was going to throw the biggest, grandest Christmas she'd ever seen. And if that didn't melt her icy heart, then she could have the inn.

But he wasn't going to back down. That wasn't his way. He would fight until his last breath.

Christmas was coming to the inn whether she liked it or not.

6

HOLLY

A sharp knock on the door drew her from her dream. A dream in which she was running through the woods but couldn't quite seem to find the way out. Trees surrounded her. The smell of pine filled her nose.

The knocking started again.

Sighing, she threw off her blankets and pushed herself up. Her feet touched the cool, hard wood floor, causing her to wince and pull her feet back. Now fully awake, she opened her eyes and glanced around.

Seven evergreen trees sat in front of her.

Well, no wonder she'd had a nightmare about running through the woods. She was literally staying in the woods.

Growling, she pushed off the bed and grabbed her robe as she tiptoed to the door. She should have known Stephen would pull something like this. Just like she should have known that he would still be here. He was never going to leave Ivy Springs—or the inn.

The knocks sounded again just as she reached the door. She unlocked the bolt and pulled the door open. Annoyed, she glanced up to see Stephen standing there with pink cheeks and wearing a red wool hat and brown coat.

"What are you doing?" she asked as she yawned and stretched. She ran her hands through her matted hair, hoping it would look natural and not like she cared that she looked a mess.

Stephen didn't wait as he pushed into her room. She sputtered a few times, but that didn't stop him. He walked over to one of the trees and loosened the bolts holding it in the tree stand. Then he bent down and hoisted the tree up onto his shoulder, sap and water dripping onto the floor.

"What are you doing still sleeping?" he asked as he made his way through the door, pausing for a moment to stare down at her.

She blinked a few times, trying to figure out what was happening. "Wha—why?" she stammered.

Stephen shifted the tree higher up onto his shoulder. "You're the owner now. You need to be up and managing the place." He reached behind him and grabbed a piece of paper from his back pocket. "Here, I made a list and everything."

He shoved the paper at her, and she scrambled to grab it. Then he smiled and pushed out into the hallway.

Desperate to save face, she followed after him. "I thought I said no Christmas decorations," she said, pressing her hands to her hips for emphasis.

Stephen chuckled. Then he turned so he could meet her gaze. "You did," he said as he winked and shrugged.

Before she could respond, he disappeared down the stairs, leaving a trail of water behind him.

Frustrated, Holly pulled her robe closed as she hurried back into her room. With the door shut and locked, she leaned against it and let out her breath.

Remembering the list that he'd shoved at her, she glanced down and unfolded it.

Room 7 has a clogged toilet

Room 9 says her room is too cold

Room 11 shoved a stuffed animal into the heater vent. It needs to be removed.

Samson isn't here to muck the stables

Groaning, she folded the paper and set it on the dresser next to her. Holding her breath, she closed her eyes as she prepared herself for what lay ahead.

She should have realized that Stephen wasn't going to make this easy on her. When she saw him standing there at the airport, she should have just turned around and went home.

She doubted that Stephen had changed since the last time they were together. When he didn't want to do something, he didn't.

Which meant she was going to suffer. He was going to make sure of it.

She knew what he was doing. He was forcing the inn on her in the hope that she would throw up her hands and leave, therefore not fulfilling the stipulation in the will. Well, he had another thing coming. She was stronger than he thought.

Plus, she doubted that he didn't have another place to store the trees he'd shoved into her room. She knew this place like the back of her hand. He was forcing Christmas on her, deliberately going against what she'd asked of him.

Well, two could play at that game. If Stephen thought he was going to break her, he'd forgotten her. She welcomed a little competition in her life.

By the time this week was over, she was going to sell this inn so fast his head would spin.

She quieted her mind as she allowed that thought to linger. Her stomach squeezed as she opened her eyes and glanced around, regret rising to the surface. The familiar floral wallpaper met her gaze as she glanced around at all the wood fixtures. Items she'd picked out with her grandmother when they had to replace broken or worn-down dressers and nightstands.

Each room held memories that made her homesick for a life

she once had and angry that the woman who'd raised her had lied to her for so long.

It was a strange having such a contrast of emotions running through her.

Not wanting to dwell on her feelings, she swallowed and pushed off the wall. She needed to focus on the list that Stephen had given her. She could sort through her emotions later when she was back in New York, debt free and preparing for the future of her relationship with Tyler.

Until then, she was in survival mode.

With a newfound determination, Holly marched into the bathroom and flipped the shower on. Ice-cold water rushed out, and Holly took her time undressing as she waited for the water to heat up.

Steam filled the room. She needed a hot shower to help relax her muscles and calm her down. Well, what she really needed was a deep tissue massage and a sauna, but there was no way she was going to get that in Ivy Springs. So a hot shower would have to do.

Five minutes into the shower with her hair suds with shampoo, the water began to sputter.

Warm then cold. Warm then cold.

Holly fiddled with the dial.

Warm. Cold. Warm.

She rushed to stick her head under the water and rinse off the soap as fast as she could. Midway through, the water sputtered and ice-cold water shot down on her.

Holly yelled as she ran her fingers through her hair, her teeth chattering. She fought the urge to jump out, still covered in soap suds.

Once the water ran clear, she smacked the dial, halting the water.

Goosebumps covered every inch of her body as she frantically grabbed a towel and began to dry off, rubbing warmth into her limbs.

She wrapped herself in her robe and her hair in a towel and made her way out of the bathroom and straight over to the heater.

Once she was warmed through, she grabbed her suitcase and hefted it onto the bed. She pulled out a T-shirt and a pair of jeans. Then she threw her hair up into a bun and put on a little makeup —not enough to look like she was trying but enough to make it look like she wasn't dead.

With her tennis shoes on and Stephen's list tucked into her back pocket, she opened her door and headed out into the hall.

The first morning of seven was done and in the books. She only had six more to go before she could leave this place and never look back.

And, with the memory of the cold shower hanging over her head, the end of the week couldn't come fast enough.

Stephen

Stephen stood in the kitchen, glancing up at the ceiling. He was busy flipping the faucet on and off.

"What are you doing?" Blossom asked as she entered the kitchen.

Startled, Stephen jumped and turned, leaving the water running. "Nothing," he said as he folded his arms and leaned his hip against the counter.

Blossom quirked an eyebrow at him. Worried that she would know what he was doing, he shrugged and gave her a big smile.

"I was just testing the faucet. Mrs. Brondy said it was leaking." He studied her for a moment, hoping she would move on or at least let up on the incredulous look she was giving him.

No such luck. Blossom continued to stare at him. "Stephen,

what's the plan here? Torture Holly enough and she'll leave?" Blossom wheeled toward him. When it became apparent that she wasn't going to stop, he jumped out of the way to avoid getting run over.

She leaned forward to try to flick off the faucet. It killed him to see his sister struggling like she was. He moved to help her, only to be stopped by her tsking.

"I'm not an invalid. Don't treat me like one," she said, extending herself enough that she finally reached the faucet and turned the water off.

"I wasn't helping," he said as he shoved his hand into the front pocket of his jeans.

Blossom sighed and settled back into her chair. She eyed him for a moment. He wanted to say something, to justify his running the hot water through the kitchen faucet when he knew it affected room thirteen's water temperature. Then he decided it was better to just pretend that he didn't know.

Blossom shook her head and folded her arms. "You know what Hope wanted. I don't understand why you're fighting this."

Stephen swallowed as he studied his sister and then blew out his breath as he nodded. "I know." He paused and shrugged. "I know. I guess I can't just rely on Hope's plan. I figured, maybe if we bug her enough, she'd leave and never look back."

Blossom raised her eyebrows. "And is that what you want?"

Stephen pinched the bridge of his nose as he closed his eyes. No. That wasn't what he wanted. But then again, he couldn't just leave his fate—and the fate of the inn—to Hope's grand plan.

It needed some intervention. A bunch of letters written to Holly didn't seem like the best path to success. Showing Holly what she missed, showing her what Christmas Inn could offer seemed like a much more solid plan.

A warm touch startled Stephen, and he opened his eyes to see that Blossom had reached out to hold his hand.

"I know what you're doing. You're a protector. But remember,

Hope knew Holly. She knew what would work. You have to trust her." Then Blossom leaned forward. "And you promised. Hope didn't seem like the kind of person to be against haunting someone."

Stephen laughed and nodded. His sister had an annoying ability to always be right.

"Okay," he said, pulling his hand away and scrubbing his face. "You're annoying. You know that, right?"

She nodded and then started to head out of the kitchen—just in time to see Holly step through the swinging doors with a somewhat startled expression. "Hey, Blossom," she said, nodding to her. His sister stopped and turned to face Stephen. Holly gave him a pained smile as she nodded in his direction.

"I'm ready," Holly said, waving toward her obvious attempt at work clothes. Her jeans looked more expensive than his truck, but he appreciated that she was taking his list seriously.

"What are you ready for?" Blossom asked as she cast her gaze between the two of them.

Not wanting her to ruin his perfect plan, Stephen stepped forward. "Holly has offered to help out around here."

"I—"

"She wants to learn the ropes before she hands the baton over to someone else," he interjected, walking over to her.

That seemed to unsettle Holly just enough for Blossom to shoot a strange look at them before wheeling herself out of the kitchen.

Now alone, Stephen patted Holly on the back and walked over to the fridge.

"Hungry?" he asked.

"Starving."

Stephen couldn't help the smile that emerged as he grabbed a carton of eggs and set them down on the counter in front of her. He then grabbed a giant silver bowl and set it next to the eggs.

"Perfect. Mrs. Brondy ran to the store and won't be back for a few hours. There are a few late guests getting up." He tapped the egg carton. "Since you're the owner…" He winked at Holly, reveling in her started expression.

"I—"

"You'll do great," he said as he made his way over to the back door and slipped on his boots. "I have a few chores out here to get to, but I'll be back." He pulled his coat on and zipped it up.

The he grabbed the keys to his truck, slipped them into his pocket, and pulled open the back door. "Have my eggs ready in thirty," he said over his shoulder. "I like them over easy."

The cool air hit every exposed bit of skin as he stepped out onto the porch and let the door swing shut on her protests.

Sure, he'd told Blossom he'd let up, and he planned to. But not before he showed Holly just how much she'd changed. The Holly he knew could handle anything, and he knew that she was still in there. She just needed some coaxing to come out. Good news for her, Stephen was more than happy to help.

He threw his truck keys into the air as his boots crunched against the compacted snow. He whistled as he made his way to his truck and climbed in.

One glance at the kitchen window showed Holly standing there, staring at something. She looked so strange. So out of place. Her lost expression tugged at his heart, just a little.

There was something so familiar about the way her blonde hair fell over her shoulders. The soft lines of her profile were etched in his memory.

He remembered touching her skin with his fingers…with his lips. It all came rushing back to him.

He sat there in his truck, allowing those thoughts to wash over him. But then, as quickly as they came, he pushed them from his mind.

The Holly he remembered wasn't the woman standing there in front of the window. That Holly was gone. And while he was

going to give reviving the girl he once loved his best shot, he
doubted it would do much.

Even if his heart hoped otherwise, his head told him the truth.
The real Holly was gone, and no amount of wishing and praying
for a Christmas miracle was going to change that.

He might as well accept it.

7

HOLLY

Holly could do this. She could.

It was making eggs, for Pete's sake. How hard could it be?

But, for some reason, she couldn't stop worrying that this was a test. That Stephen had asked her to do these things to see if she could still hack it in Ivy Springs. That he thought she'd become too soft while being away.

If she was being honest, she couldn't remember the last time she'd used her stove. Why would she when there was a restaurant or food truck around every corner in New York? Plus, Tyler loved to eat out, and Holly was always happy to oblige.

Holly huffed as she glanced around, trying to figure out where Mrs. Brondy would have stored the frying pans.

After opening just about every cupboard, she found the pans and pulled one out. She set it on a burner and turned the knob.

There, easy enough.

"What are you doing?" a small voice said behind her.

Holly yelped and turned to see Isaac standing behind her. He had tousled hair and pink cheeks like he'd just been running around. His eyes were wide as he studied her.

"Mrs. Brondy doesn't like it when we play in the kitchen." He rose up onto his tiptoes and glanced into the pan. Then he looked over at her. "Can I help?"

She studied him with her brow furrowed. He was a cute enough kid. And when she saw Stephen playing with him last night—well, she was a woman. She doubted there was a female person in the dining room last night that hadn't been affected by watching a handsome man care for his nephew.

Clearing her throat, she shoved all thoughts of Stephen from her thoughts and smiled at Isaac. "Do you know how to crack eggs?" she asked as she motioned to the egg carton.

His eyes widened as he glanced up at her. "You mean I can..." His voice drifted off as his expression turned reverent and he crossed his hands over his chest. "I will do my best."

Holly laughed and walked over to the bar to grab a stool. "Well, you can't do any worse than me."

Isaac bobbed his head with glee, and as soon as she situated the stool in front of the stove, he climbed right up.

"The key is cracking the egg on the side of the pan," she said as she handed him an egg. "Hang on, though. We need butter."

Isaac cradled the egg in his palm and settled back on the stool. Holly reached out and held her hand over the pan to feel how hot it was.

But no heat was rising from the pan.

Confused, she glanced at the knobs and fiddled with them again. She had no idea how to use this stove, so she glanced around the kitchen and zeroed in on the microwave. All right, it was time to pivot. She flipped off the burner.

After scouring the kitchen, she came up with a few porcelain bowls. "We are going to use these," she said, winking at Isaac.

In no time, they had the eggs cracked and beaten. Then Holly nodded toward the microwave as she carried a bowl in each hand.

It didn't take long before all the eggs were fully cooked.

Though the jury was still out on whether they were edible. She was starving.

Just as she set the bowls on the small round table in the corner, the back door opened and Stephen came in. His hair was wind-blown, and the tip of his nose and his cheeks were bright pink. He pulled off his hat and dusted it off as he stomped his boots.

"Steppen!" Isaac exclaimed as he rushed over and jumped into Stephen's arms.

Stephen laughed and hugged Isaac. Feeling as if she were intruding on their moment, she turned back to the table and focused on setting forks next to the bowls.

"I helped Holly cook," Isaac said.

Holly could hear Stephen's footsteps as he came closer.

"Cook?" he asked.

Frustrated, she turned around, but instead of a teasing look, Stephen looked grateful.

"I, um...I couldn't figure out how to get the stove to work, so we improvised."

Stephen studied the eggs and then glanced over at Holly. "And you let Isaac help?" he asked just as Isaac wiggled for Stephen to allow him to slip to the floor. Stephen shoved his hands into his front pockets as he kept his gaze on her face.

Heat rose up inside of her and settled in her cheeks. She hoped he would assume it was from the temperature of the room and not from the fact that his stare was doing strange things to her insides.

"He's a good helper," she said as she shrugged.

Stephen held her gaze for a moment before he nodded. "He's a good kid." He reached out and ruffled Isaac's hair. Isaac, in turn, reached out and swatted Stephen's hand away.

"Plus, he seems to be loving the eggs," Stephen said as he chuckled and nodded toward Isaac, who had already eaten half his bowl. Then he grabbed a chair and took a seat at the table.

Not sure what to do, Holly just stood there, feeling like an idiot. Then she picked up one of the bowls and nodded toward the dining room. "Should I go put this out there? You know, for the guests?"

Stephen shoved a forkful of eggs into his mouth as he glanced up at her. After chewing, he shook his head. "I think we should leave these for us," he said with a wink.

She hated that the playful hint to his voice sent shivers down her back. Or the fact that he was teasing her. It was almost like he was trying to be friends again. As if that would make her change her mind about the inn.

But she wasn't going to. No matter how many sexy smiles he cast her way or how adorable his nephew was. When she set her mind to something, she did it.

They sat in silence as they devoured the eggs. They weren't fabulous, but they weren't terrible either. Considering she'd had to improvise when she couldn't figure out how to use the stove, she was pretty proud of herself.

"That wasn't too bad," Stephen said as he finished his eggs and leaned back in his chair, rubbing his stomach for emphasis.

Holly took her last bite and then reached out to take his bowl. Stephen must have had the same idea because his fingers brushed hers. They were warm, and before Holly started dissecting Stephen's intentions, she yanked her hand back as if she'd been burned.

"Sorry," she mumbled, pushing her chair back and hurrying to the sink to rinse out her bowl.

Isaac declared that he was done, and in the blink of an eye, he'd escaped through the swinging kitchen door.

Now alone with Stephen, Holly tried to busy herself at the sink, hoping that if she stared hard enough at the faucet, Stephen would think she was deep in thought and leave her alone.

No such luck.

"You okay?" Stephen's voice was deep and close—really close.

A shiver ran up her spine as she hushed her pounding heart.

Only an idiot would allow themself to entertain the old feelings that were bubbling up inside of her.

"Yeah, I'm okay," she whispered.

He set his bowl down next to her. Then, from the corner of her eye, she saw him lean against the counter and fold his arms. He took a deep breath. "This isn't easy for me," he said slowly, his voice deep.

She closed her eyes for a moment before she turned the faucet off. She dried her hands and tucked the towel onto the dishwasher's handle then turned her attention to Stephen.

When she met his gaze, her breath caught in her throat. There were those bright green eyes. The ones she'd gotten lost in all those years ago. She would never grow tired of getting lost in the depths of them. They were so familiar. Like a song she knew the words to without even hearing the music.

And she doubted she would ever stop feeling that way toward Stephen. He was her first love. He would always hold a place in her heart. But that didn't change why she was here. What she had to do. It never would.

"I know it's not," she said as she threaded her fingers together in front of her, glancing down every so often—just to give herself a break from staring into his eyes.

He sighed and scrubbed his face. "But that's not going to change anything, is it?" he asked, the question coming out as more of a statement.

She didn't want to hurt his feelings, but she was a woman on a mission. He should have known that.

"I'm sorry, Stephen," she whispered. A little taken aback by her own emotions. She knew she cared, she just hadn't realized how much.

But she couldn't allow herself to care for him or the inn. Not today. Not this week. Her feelings only got her in trouble. That's why she was thankful for Tyler. That relationship made sense.

Then she shook her head. What was she thinking? She didn't

have a relationship with Stephen anymore, and she didn't want one. Did she?

Ugh. Coming to Christmas Inn had been a mistake. A huge, colossal mistake.

Needing to get out of there, she shot Stephen a smile—so he wouldn't see her insane reaction—and turned to head out of the kitchen.

"Holly," Stephen said, his hand finding her arm.

She paused, trying to figure out how to respond and decided it was best to just stand there and wait.

When he didn't continue, her breath caught in her throat. What did this mean? Did she want to know?

"I was just wondering..." he started. The way he was drawing out his words was killing her.

She allowed herself to look up and meet his gaze. He held it for a moment before he parted his lips.

"I was wondering what's wrong with the stove?"

His tone was so tender that it took her a moment to realize what he had actually asked.

"What?"

He tipped his head toward the stove as he dropped his hand from her arm. "The stove. What's wrong with it?"

Holly blinked. "It wouldn't heat up," she said, feeling like an idiot.

He raised his eyebrows. "It's not heating up? Mrs. Brondy didn't say anything to me this morning." He made his way over to the stove.

Feeling as if her intelligence was being questioned, Holly followed after him. "Well, I turned the dial and nothing happened," she said, waving toward the dial she'd used.

Stephen leaned closer, his fingers gripping the dial. The movement caused his chest to brush her arm, and tingles erupted across her skin.

Blast.

"Did you light the pilot?" he asked.

"What?"

He glanced down at her. He hadn't moved away. Not even an inch. Instead, he remained so close she could smell his laundry detergent mixed with the scent of the outdoors. It was woodsy and clean and was causing her head to spin.

"Holly, you have to light the pilot or all you're doing is running gas." He glanced around the room—still not moving to step back. "I'm just glad you didn't blow the room up," he said as he glanced down at her and, of course, gave her a wink.

Embarrassment and frustration coursed through her as she growled and stepped away. "Why do you keep doing that?" she asked before she even realized she was speaking. Her cheeks burned as she pinched her lips together and closed her eyes.

"Do what?" Stephen asked. His eyebrows were raised as he studied her.

"Wink at me," she whispered.

His chuckle was soft as he swept his gaze from side to side, finally allowing it to land on her. "Does it bother you?"

No, it confused her. But she wasn't going to say that. "It's not very professional."

Stephen's eyes widened. "I didn't realize we had a professional kind of relationship."

Holly nodded as she attempted to redeem herself. Why hadn't she just kept her lips shut? She doubted that there weren't too many women who visited Christmas Inn that would be bothered by the ridiculously good-looking manager winking at them.

And now that she'd confessed her issue, was he going to read into it?

Suddenly, Stephen's hand was on her shoulder, drawing her from her spiral. "I'll stop winking at you if it bothers you that much," he said and offered her a comforting smile.

Holly's breath caught in her throat as she studied him for a moment and then nodded. "That would be great." Her gaze trailed down to his hand on her shoulder. It was warm and familiar and caused shivers to erupt across her skin.

It took Stephen a few seconds to pull his hand away. Almost as if he'd forgotten that he was touching her. She offered him a soft smile as he brought his hand up and run it through his hair.

"I should get going. I've got lots to do," he said, nodding toward the back door.

Holly lifted up the list that Stephen had given her earlier. "Me too," she said, waving it in front of her.

"You don't—"

"I do," Holly said. She wanted to change the way he saw her. She was here to do a job. Not to reconnect with her ex.

Which was ridiculous to even think. Especially when she was dating someone else.

Stephen studied her for a moment before he pulled on his outerwear and slipped outside, shutting the door behind him.

Now alone, Holly sighed as she folded her arms and leaned her hip against the counter. Well she'd survived that—just barely. Pinching the bridge of her nose, she took in a deep breath and attempted to calm her nerves. She could do this. She was strong.

All she needed to do was stay ahead of her feelings and she just might make it out of this Christmas holiday with her emotions intact. And with the way she was feeling, she'd call that a win.

8

STEPHEN

S tephen spent the whole day avoiding going inside. Well, really he was avoiding Holly.

After he tried to open up to her that morning. To let his guard down and remind her that he wasn't the bad guy—even though he hadn't really sided with her during her falling out with Hope. She had shot him down.

He was such an idiot to think that things could be different. That he'd be able to change her mind with a few flirty conversations and a smile.

Only a fool would think that was all it took to thaw a frozen heart.

As the sun began to set behind the trees, Stephen walked across the patio and up the porch stairs, shivering. Tonight, they were going to decorate the Christmas trees that he'd picked up from town.

He'd felt bad about stuffing all the trees in Holly's room, which was why he'd started taking them out that morning. But after their interaction at breakfast, he wasn't interested in helping her out anymore. She deserved to have some Christmas cheer in her room, so he'd decided to leave them there.

He stomped the snow off his boots and pulled open the door that led into the kitchen. Warmth and the smell of Mrs. Brondy's potpie surrounded him and made his heart sing.

He loved this time of year. The time when the inn was packed with family and those who cherished the holiday season.

And no stick-in-the-mud grinch was going to change that.

"Well, where have you been?" Mrs. Brondy asked, appearing from behind the open fridge door.

Stephen chuckled as he pulled off his gloves, shoved them into his coat pocket, and then hung his coat on the hook. After kicking off his boots, he removed his hat and tousled his hair, which sticking up from static electricity.

"I was getting stuff done around the stalls," he replied. Sure, the fence could have been fixed come summer. And the squeaky hinges didn't need WD-40 just now, but he needed jobs outside of the inn, so he was going to do them.

Mrs. Brondy studied him from above her readers. She had a skeptical expression. Her lips were pinched, and a soft "mm-hmm" sounded from her throat.

Stephen winked, grabbed a roll that was cooling on the rack next to him, and ducked to avoid the dish towel Mrs. Brondy sent his way.

"Thanks," he said over his shoulder as he took a bite of the roll and slipped through the swinging kitchen door and right into a very surprised Holly.

He rammed right into her. And as she started to fall, he wrapped his arm around her waist and pulled her to him, crushing her against his body.

His entire soul warmed as he stared down into her wide eyes. Then, realizing what he was doing, he righted her and stepped back. "Sorry," he mumbled as he shuffled to the side and ducked past her. There was no way he was going to stand there while she stared at him.

"Stephen?" Holly called after him, halting his retreat.

He paused. He really wasn't interested in talking to her right now. If fact, he was fine with spending the rest of the holiday season avoiding her. Staying away from her was going to keep his heart intact, that much he knew.

But he couldn't just walk away. There was an actual tug inside of his chest that was pulling him toward her.

"Yep?" he asked. And as he turned, he took in her physical appearance.

Her hair was pulled up into a messy bun at the top of her head. Her cheeks were pink, and, from the wild look in her eyes, it had to be from exertion. Add to that her wrinkled t-shirt and frumpy pants, and he couldn't help but smile.

For a woman who seemed to have her life together, she looked like a hot mess. An adorable, annoyingly beautiful hot mess.

Holly didn't seem to notice his sudden brain halt. She marched over to him and shoved the list he'd given her into his hand. "Finished," she said.

The tone in her voice surprised him. Instead of confident or business-like, her tone was celebratory. Almost as if she had doubted that completing the list was something she could do.

"Really?" he asked. He unfolded the piece of paper and glanced down to see tiny check marks next to each of the items.

When he glanced back up, he saw Holly nodding as she chewed her lip.

"Well, I didn't get to the stalls, but I'm headed there right now." She blew away a few strands of hair that had floated down over her face.

Stephen couldn't ignore the desire to help her that was growing inside of him. So he shoved the list into his pocket and nodded toward the kitchen. "Come on, we can do it together," he said, not waiting to hear her response.

Honestly, it didn't matter. He was going to help her whether she wanted him to or not.

Thankfully, she just followed him through the kitchen to the back door. Stephen pulled open the small closet next to the door and began to rummage around, looking for some older winter wear items she could borrow.

"Put these on," he said as he pulled out a coat, a pair of boots, and gloves.

Holly's eyes widened as her gaze swept over the items. "I'm good."

Stephen snorted. "Put them on. I'm not giving you my coat if we get out there and it's too cold for you," he said as he held up the jacket and shook it in front of her.

Holly chewed her lip and then sighed, muttering under her breath that she was in the middle of nowhere and that none of her clients would see her.

Stephen bit his tongue to keep from responding as he slid on his own outerwear. Why did it matter what she looked like? She needed to stay warm. He sighed as he watched her slip the boots and gloves on. She'd changed so much and yet looked so familiar. It was a strange push and pull as he watched her.

"What?" she asked, stopping to stare at him.

Stephen cleared his throat as he straightened. Then he shook his head, hoping that she wouldn't read into his gaze. "You've just changed. That's all."

Holly pulled her hair out from under her coat and then slid the zipper up. "Well, I grew up, Stephen. What do you want me to say?"

Stephen scoffed as he leaned forward and twisted the door handle. After he pulled open the door, he nodded toward the outside. The sun had set, and darkness fell around. He'd strung lights on the trellises that surrounded the patio. They lit up the snow as it swirled around on the wind.

It was like they were living in a snow globe. If he wasn't walking behind Holly, who seemed to confuse and frustrate him at every turn, it might actually have been a peaceful experience.

But with the wave of emotions running through him, he was anything but calm.

When they got to the stables, he pushed open the door and Holly walked inside. He followed after her, shutting the door to keep the cold wind at bay. He flipped on the lights and the radio turned on as well.

Soft Christmas music played throughout the space.

He winced as he muttered an apology and headed toward the radio to turn it off.

"It's okay," Holly said as she glanced around.

Stephen turned, startled that she was actually allowing some Christmas cheer in her vicinity. But when he caught sight of her expression, he paused.

She looked sad as she walked over to one of the horses and placed her hand on its nose. The gelding nuzzled it for a moment and then returned to eating from the bucket of hay that Stephen had rigged on the door. Holly laughed and patted his neck.

It was in that moment he saw the girl he'd once loved. The gentleness to her form. He could hear her soft whispers as she leaned in to speak to the horse.

Holly had always loved riding, and they had spent many nights riding through the surrounding woods together during their high school years. They would find forgotten or undiscovered spots where they would tie the horses up and stay for hours, just the two of them.

It was in those moments that they would talk about their greatest fears. Their worries. Stephen would wrap his arms around Holly and tell her that he was never going to let her go.

They would plan what their life would look like in the future. They talked about marriage. About kids.

The warmth from those memories burned in Stephen's stomach and he cursed himself for allowing it.

Why couldn't his mind and body realize that the past was only good if it stayed in the past. Standing there, allowing himself to imagine what might have happened was foolish.

So he forced the thoughts from his mind as he walked over to the shovels and wheelbarrow.

"Let's get this over with," he said, handing a shovel to Holly.

She stepped back from the horse and glanced over at Stephen. She looked startled—as if she'd forgotten what she was there for. Her gaze roamed over him and then over to the shovel he was holding. She nodded and took it from him.

They worked across from each other, mucking the stalls and not talking.

Desperate to break the silence between them, Stephen asked, "Do you do a lot of riding?" He scooped up some bedding and dumped it into the wheelbarrow.

From the corner of his eye, he saw Holly pause and glance over at him.

"No. I haven't gone riding in a long time," she said, a forlorn hint to her voice.

It intrigued him, so he paused and turned to study her. He leaned against his shovel as he raised his eyebrows. Holly looked as if she weren't done talking, and she looked so full of regret, he wasn't going to stop her.

He'd always assumed that the life she'd picked over him had made her happier than she would have been in Ivy Springs. It might sound selfish, but the fact that, perhaps, that wasn't the case, made him feel better. At least for a moment.

Until he saw the true pain in her gaze.

That wasn't what he wanted for her. So, he shot her a smile. "Well it's a good thing you're here. These horses could definitely use a break from these stalls." He moved to pat Daisy, the horse he was standing next to, on the nose. She nudged him a few times before returning to the hay.

"That would be nice," Holly said, drawing his attention back over to her.

He studied her for a moment. He had so many questions, but he just didn't know how to ask any of them.

Why would she stay away if she was so unhappy? He knew Hope had hurt her, but at some point she had to move on, right? Hadn't the thought of missing her grandmother—of missing him —bothered her at all? He knew Holly. And staying away for years wasn't like her. She was gentle and kind and nothing like this hardened exterior she'd put on.

But how could he ask questions like that? If he bared his soul to Holly, how did he know she wasn't going to turn and run away?

"There's not a lot of grass in New York," she said as she sighed and leaned against the handle of her shovel. Her gaze roamed around the stalls, and from the soft expression on her face, he could tell she wasn't thinking such heavy thoughts like he was.

And that made him a tad jealous. Why did he always overthink things? Holly leaving was eating him up inside, and yet, she didn't seem bothered at all.

"That must have been a shock, moving to a big city like that," he said. It was probably best for him to return to working. After all, it wasn't doing him any good to stand there and delve into the past. Especially when her thoughts were clearly not moving in the same direction.

She chuckled. It was soft and sweet. "Yeah, it was hard. Especially after growing up surrounded by so much nature. In New York, the only things that are tall are the buildings." She sighed. "I missed these woods."

Stephen's heart picked up speed at her words. Hearing that she missed something about this place brought him hope. Maybe if she remembered the things she loved about growing up in Ivy Springs, she wouldn't sell the inn.

"Maybe it'd be a good thing to keep this place around, huh? Think of how many people need an escape from their busy lives in the city." He hoped he came across as nonchalant, even though he felt increasingly desperate. He was ready to do anything to keep her from selling this place.

Holly paused and glanced up at him. Her expression was hard to read, and it made him twitch. Had he said the wrong thing? He was hoping to capitalize on her nostalgia, but now he was worried he'd misread the situation. He could feel her pulling away.

"That's not fair," she said as she grabbed the handle of the shovel and began sifting through the bedding.

"I'm sorry, Holly," he said. The words were true. He didn't want to hurt her. But that didn't mean he wasn't going to challenge her. After all, he had people to protect. Lives that depended on him.

He couldn't just ignore those responsibilities. Even though a part of him wanted to protect Holly. To make sure she didn't hurt as much as she obviously was.

He got back to work, his mind chewing on his thoughts as he decided what to say next. Hope's letter that he had stashed in his room floated into his mind.

"Before you go to bed tonight, come to my room. I have something for you," he blurted out. The words shot from his lips before he could stop them.

Holly stopped working and glanced over at him. When she didn't say anything right away, he feared that he might have said the wrong thing. He got ready to backtrack, but then she nodded.

"Okay," she said.

He raised his eyebrows. "Okay?" he repeated and then felt like an idiot.

She nodded. "Okay."

Feeling confident again, he smiled and nodded—and almost winked, but he caught himself. Holly gave him a small smile and returned to mucking out the stalls. Stephen did the same, ready to lose himself in the monotony of shoveling.

At least here, he didn't have to agonize over what he'd said. Or what Holly wasn't saying. Or how much his heart quickened at his memories of her.

In work, his heart was safe. And he couldn't risk losing his heart again. Especially when it felt like he'd never fully gotten it back.

9

HOLLY

Dinner was delicious. The potpie that Mrs. Brondy made had the flakiest crust and creamiest gravy Holly had ever eaten. Add that to the ambiance of the evening, and Holly was feeling quite at home.

She leaned back in her chair and stretched her arms over her head.

This dinner was exactly what she needed. Especially after her semi-confusing conversation with Stephen out in the stables. He'd been so open and willing to share one moment and then closed off and cold the next.

She was trying to figure out why it bothered her so much, yet she couldn't quite dissect it. So she chalked it up to their history and pushed it from her mind.

Glancing around the room, she saw him sitting with Blossom and Isaac. His eyes were wide as he nodded at Isaac, whose excitement could be seen from across the room.

He was a cute kid. And the fact that he had Stephen enthralled with whatever he was saying...well, it made Holly long for a similar relationship.

She'd spent most of her life thinking she didn't need anyone.

People only hurt her. But the more she was around Stephen and his nephew, the more she was beginning to realize that maybe she was wrong.

Sure, she had the life she'd always thought she wanted. New York City. A somewhat blossoming career. Parties on the weekend. Fancy dinners with fabulous wine.

All of it was exactly what she wanted. What she'd left Ivy Springs in search of. But she was finding it harder and harder to convince herself that she was actually happy.

Groaning, she rested her elbows on the table and buried her face in her hands. She took in a few deep breaths and stilled her mind. That was why she hadn't wanted to come back here. She was already starting to question the life she'd built for herself.

All she needed to do was force herself to remember the reasons why she'd left. Then she would remember why living in Ivy Springs hurt so much.

A moment later, her phone rang. She sat up and shifted in her seat so she could pull it from her back pocket. An unknown number flashed across the screen.

Hoping that it was Tyler—she could use the distraction—Holly stood up, pushed her chair in, and hurried from the room. Just as she passed by Stephen's table, she felt his gaze on her.

But she didn't look at him. She made her way out into the foyer and settled down in front of the bay window.

"Hello?" she asked after she pressed the green talk button and brought her phone to her ear.

"Hello?" Tyler's voice was muffled, and static filled the silence.

"Hello? Tyler?"

"Holly?"

"Yeah, I'm here," she said, trying not to shout into the phone.

"Hang on." There were some muffled sounds as he shifted around. Then, suddenly, the connection got better. "Holly?" Tyler's voice was smooth and just what she needed to calm her ragged nerves.

"Yes, it's me." She pulled her feet up onto the bench and hugged her knees to her chest. She tipped her head back to rest on the window frame behind her.

"What's wrong?"

She closed her eyes for a moment as she contemplated how to answer that question. Nothing was going according to plan. She felt so out of place. Like she didn't belong here or in New York.

There were fleeting moments when she was reminded of everything she'd given up, but then seeing how little Christmas Inn had changed since she left made her feel lost and confused. She wished she could just go back to New York and live her very predictable life again.

But telling all of that to Tyler wasn't going to help her feel better. He didn't need to be bogged down by her issues.

"Everything's fine. I've just been helping out a lot around here. Fixing clogged toilets. Stuff like that."

Tyler snorted. "Toilets? You fixed toilets?"

She pinched her lips together and nodded. "Yeah."

"They don't have a handyman there?"

She swallowed as her thoughts instantly turned to Stephen. He was a detail she was going to leave out of this conversation. After all, in a week, this place would be sold, and Stephen would be just a distant memory.

It wasn't that Tyler was the jealous type. But if he heard that she was spending pretty much every day with her ex, he probably wasn't going to be too happy.

"Yeah, but it's the busy time of year. He's got lots to do as well."

Tyler clicked his tongue. "Well, make sure he's doing his job. There shouldn't be any reason for the owner to do that kind of work." He paused. "Do you want me to talk to him?"

Holly straightened and shook her head. "Oh no. It's fine. I've talked to him. He understands."

Tyler hesitated. "Well, if he gives you any trouble, you let me know. I can be very persuasive."

"I know. And in under a week, the inn will be sold, and it won't be a problem anymore. I can hold out for a week."

"That's right. There's light at the end of the tunnel." There was a muffled conversation on his end, and then Tyler said, "I've gotta go."

Holly tried not to protest. It was nice to hear his voice. "All right. I love you," she said just as the phone clicked and the call ended. Holly pulled her phone from her ear and glanced at the screen.

Tyler had hung up.

Sighing, she set her phone down next to her and tipped her head back to rest on the frame once more. She glanced out at the falling snow. It was relaxing.

"Who was that?" Blossom's soft voice asked from behind her.

Holly startled as she glanced over to see Blossom had wheeled up next to her. She hugged her knees and rested her chin on them. "Tyler, my boyfriend."

Blossom raised her eyebrows. "Your boyfriend?"

Holly nodded. "We've been dating for a few years now."

Right on cue, Blossom's gaze dipped down to Holly's left hand. It was the normal response she got when people found out how long they had been dating.

"Just boyfriend?" Blossom asked—obviously wanting to ask a different question.

Holly shrugged. "He's a surgeon and wants to get established. We both work all the time." She swung her feet to the ground.

Blossom nodded. "And where is he now?"

Holly slipped her phone into her back pocket. "He's in Africa with Doctors Without Borders."

"So he's not coming?"

Holly shook her head. "No."

Silence fell around them. Blossom studied Holly, which made her a tad uncomfortable.

"Just be careful," Blossom said as she folded her hands in her lap.

Confused, Holly furrowed her brow. "With what?"

Blossom pinched her lips together and Holly could see her indecisiveness. Like she wanted to say something but didn't know how. Finally, Blossom sighed. "Stephen doesn't deserve to get hurt again," she said.

Holly could hear the bite in her tone. At first, she wasn't sure what to think about it, but then she realized that Blossom was always going to protect her brother. And, honestly, Holly didn't want to hurt Stephen either.

But she couldn't hold onto a business she didn't want just to spare someone's feelings. "I know," Holly said.

Just as Blossom's expression turned to one of satisfaction, Holly added, "But I still plan on selling Christmas Inn." She slowly raised her gaze to see that Blossom's smile had faded.

She held Holly's gaze for a moment before she sighed and nodded. "I understand, even if Stephen doesn't." With that, she turned back to the reception desk.

Now alone, Holly stood and wrapped her arms around her chest. A feeling of unease rose up inside of her.

Selling Christmas Inn had seemed so easy when it was just this abstract place that stood between her and paying off her debt. Now, she was beginning to remember that it was a home. That people depended on it.

Holly shook her head as she made her way to her room and shut the door behind her. She flopped down on her bed and groaned.

This was why she'd stayed away from the place. Opening herself up to those who lived here had only got her in trouble before. Sure, Blossom was protecting Stephen, but had she forgotten the pain Holly went through here? The secrets that were kept from her.

Even though it was hard, she knew Christmas Inn had to be

sold, no matter what. And building a relationship with the man in charge of the inn was out of the question.

She needed to be on her guard around him. She knew Stephen. She knew how persuasive he could be. If she was going to keep her head, she needed to stay away from him.

No matter what.

———

Holly started awake the next morning, the memory of her and Stephen in the barn fresh in her mind. He'd asked her to come to his room after dinner, yet she'd fallen asleep fully clothed on top of her bedding.

Frustrated, she groaned as she made her way into the bathroom and stared at her reflection in the mirror. She'd been so distracted by her conversation with Blossom that she'd completely forgot, and now she felt like an idiot.

After she brushed her teeth, washed off her makeup, and threw her hair up into a messy bun at the top of her head, she changed into a loose sweatshirt and jeans. She slipped on her tennis shoes and jacket and then made her way out into the hallway, locking the door behind her.

The caretaker of Christmas Inn had always lived in the small building just to the south of the stables. That's where she figured she'd find Stephen.

Luckily, the sun was just starting to rise over the horizon and the entire inn was silent as she walked down the stairs, through the dining room, and into the kitchen. She zipped up her jacket and tucked her chin down inside the collar as she pulled the door open and stepped out into the chilly morning air.

Her breath puffed in front of her as she closed the door and shoved her hands into her pockets. The wind blew around her, cutting through her jeans and chilling her bones. She hurried across the patio and past the stables. As soon as she got to the caretaker's house, she rapped on the door.

The lights were still off, so she pounded harder. Either Stephen was asleep, or he wasn't there. Her nose felt as if it were freezing off her face.

Just as she moved to pound the door again, it swung open, revealing a shirtless, angry Stephen. He'd opened the door so fast, that in the absence of something to stop her hand, she stumbled forward—right into Stephen's muscular and very warm chest.

Heat permeated her body as she glanced up and saw that his expression had turned from frustration to amusement.

"I'm sorry," she stammered as she shifted to stand.

It may have been her imagination, but Stephen didn't let her go as quickly as she expected. Instead, his arms remained wrapped around her for a few seconds before he helped her up.

Now that the shock of seeing Stephen shirtless had worn off, Holly committed herself to keep her gaze at eye level and not allow it to slip down. Her skin already felt as if it were going to catch on fire—no need to give it more kindling.

Stephen ran his hands through his hair as he glanced behind her. "Is the inn on fire? Why on earth did you wake me up this early?" He moved his gaze back to her, and despite the fact that it was cold enough to freeze your face off, Holly melted a bit.

Holly shivered as she tucked her coat in around her. Stephen must have noticed because he stepped to the side and waved her in.

She nodded, and just as she passed by him, her arm brushed his chest. Sure, her arm was protected by layers of fabric, but there was something inside of her stomach that took flight. She wouldn't call them butterflies, because that would mean Stephen had an effect on her. And she couldn't have that.

So she pushed those silly thoughts from her mind as she made a beeline for the couch and plopped down on it.

Stephen had shut the door and was standing in the entryway

with a confused look on his face. His arms were crossed in front of him, and Holly tried really hard to not appreciate the way his forearms looked. His skinny, teenage body had been replaced by a man's one. Stephen had changed a lot since she last saw him. And not in the hairy, beer belly way.

"What are you doing here?" he asked again.

Holly sat up, resting her hands on her knees. She parted her lips only to have her gaze slip down to his chest again. "Can you get dressed?" she asked, hoping he wouldn't notice the desperation in her voice.

He studied her. "Why? It's not like you've never seen my chest before."

Heat settled in her cheeks as memories splashed into her mind. Memories that she had no intention of reliving.

"Yeah, well, that was a long time ago. We work together now." She hoped she sounded cool and collected, because inside, she was a raging mess.

Stephen narrowed his eyes and then he sighed. "Well, if we were just coworkers, then you wouldn't be barging into my house at the crack of dawn." He shot her a look as he walked across the living room and headed into the room at the back.

Holly couldn't help but wonder if that was his bedroom. Then, when her body reacted to that thought, she pushed it from her mind and decided to think about rodents with the hope that something that disgusted her would help lower her body temperature.

She shouldn't be entertaining those sorts of feelings for her ex.

When Stephen reemerged, he was fully dressed. His hair was damp as if he'd wetted it down with water. He walked past her into the tiny kitchen and started making coffee. Holly stood and wandered over to the card table that was next to the kitchen.

Stephen held up his hand as he pulled open a cupboard. "Coffee first," he mumbled.

As soon as the pot was full, he poured two cups and brought

her one. "Sorry, I don't have cream or sugar," he said as he sat down on one of the mismatched chairs.

Holly shrugged and sat down next to him. Her knee bumped his and he shifted away. "Sorry," she muttered.

A pained look passed over Stephen's face, but he just shrugged. "No worries. I don't break." He shot her a smile as he rested his arm on the tabletop and began to drum his fingers.

"So?" he asked, raising his eyebrows as he studied her. "I'm guessing this isn't payback for what I did to you yesterday."

Holly furrowed her brow, and then she remembered Stephen barreling into her room to get a tree. She shook her head as she wrapped her hands around the mug, enjoying the warmth. "No. I forgot to come over last night." She glanced up at him. "I guess I wanted to catch you before you left for the day."

Stephen remained quiet as he studied her. Then he took another sip and set the mug down on the table, his lips tipping up into a smile. "You were worried about me?"

Holly sputtered. "That's not what I meant at all. I just...I just didn't want to..."

What? What was she supposed to say? Everything that was coming to mind just made her sound dumb.

Suddenly, Stephen reached over and engulfed her hand in his. "I'm joking, Holly." His voice had deepened and was causing goosebumps to race across her skin.

She glanced up at him and held his gaze for a moment. All forms of speech left her mind as she allowed herself to disappear into the depths of his green eyes.

Then, realizing that she was headed into dangerous territory, she pulled her hand away and shoved it into her jacket pocket. "You told me you had something for me yesterday."

Stephen looked at her for a moment before he nodded. "Yes," he said. He stood and walked over to the fridge. Then he reached forward and removed an envelope from under a magnet. "A letter. From Hope." He handed it over to her and returned to his seat.

Holly stared at it. It was such a contrast of emotions. She'd just gone from confusing butterflies to a rock in her stomach in five seconds flat. She stared at the note her grandmother had written for her.

"Oh," she whispered. Knowing that it would be rude to refuse it, she grabbed the envelope and shoved it into her pocket. Then she stood. "Is that it?"

Stephen was studying her with an intrigued expression. When she raised her eyebrows, prompting him to speak, he just nodded.

"Okay," she said as she stepped past him and over to the front door. She didn't wait for him to respond. Instead, she pulled open the door and stepped back out into the cold.

This time, she welcomed the chill. She needed a cold slap in the face to distract her from the emotions that were swirling around inside of her mind. There was too much to unpack, and if she wanted to leave Christmas Inn with her heart intact, she needed to get her head on straight.

Before it was too late.

10

STEPHEN

Stephen spent the morning trying to push down all the thoughts and feelings that were creeping up inside of him. He wasn't sure what to make of any of them.

From Holly blushing at seeing him without his shirt on to the way her face fell when he handed her the letter from Hope—all of it was making him confused and frustrated.

He hated seeing Holly hurt, but he just didn't know how to help her.

He spent the morning in the stalls, feeding and watering the horses. After he brushed them, he gave them fresh bedding and then headed into the inn for lunch.

Thankfully, Holly seemed determined to stay away from him. He hadn't seen her all day—even though his ears perked at every sound and his heart took off running when he thought it might be her.

By the time he sat down at the table next to Isaac with a huge deli sandwich and some fries from Mrs. Brondy, he was a wreck. Why he'd let Holly get under his skin was beyond him. He should have known better. He should have worked harder at keeping his distance. Now he was playing defense when he should have been playing offense.

"We haven't seen you all morning," Blossom said as she lifted her sandwich to her lips.

Stephen had a mouthful of fries, so he just nodded. Once he swallowed, he downed his glass of water and tried to still his nerves. "I was working."

"You seem to be doing a lot of working outside lately," she said, making a point to stare at something just over his shoulder. "Is there anything you want to talk to me about?"

Stephen knew who she was looking at, but he couldn't help himself. He glanced behind him to see Holly sitting alone at the table in the far corner. She had an open book and a half-eaten sandwich in front of her.

Growling, Stephen dropped his gaze and focused back on his plate. "It's nothing I can't handle."

"She has a boyfriend, you know that, right?"

Stephen paused mid-bite to stare at his sister. Rage rose up inside of him. Thoughts about whether the guy was treating her right flew into his mind, surprising even him.

He shrugged and bit into his sandwich. He tried to play it off like he didn't care, but from his sister's raised eyebrows, it was clear she didn't believe him.

"So," he finally said, speaking around a mouthful of meat and bread.

Blossom folded her arms across her chest. "Stephen, you can't do this. You can't go down this path again." Blossom grabbed a fry, but instead of eating it she twirled it between her fingers.

"Mommy, don't play with your food," Isaac said.

Remembering that his nephew was next to him, Stephen turned to focus his attention on something other than his sister's prying gaze. He was ready to stop talking about Holly. Heck, he was ready to stop thinking about her.

Isaac glanced up at him as he bounced on his knees. He shoved a few more fries into his mouth and grinned.

"Wanna do something fun today?" Stephen asked as he winked at his nephew.

Isaac let out a hoot, and half the dining room glanced over at them. Stephen shot them an apologetic look as he shushed Isaac. "Not so loud, buddy," he said.

Isaac shushed himself and nodded. "I wanna do something fun. I'm bored."

Stephen smiled. "Great. I was thinking we've got some trees to decorate."

Isaac pumped his fists in the air. "Yes!"

They both finished off their food in record time. For Isaac, it was from his excitement. For Stephen, it had more to do with avoiding talking to his sister—a fact that she seemed to pick up on.

They cleared their plates and set them in the kitchen, and then Stephen moved to pick up Isaac. But he'd disappeared.

"Isaac?" he called out as he glanced around the kitchen. When he came up empty, he pushed through into the dining room. It only took a second to locate him.

Isaac had, of course, climbed up onto the chair next to Holly and was chatting with her. Holly's smile was genuine—probably the first one he'd seen since she'd been there. She tucked her hair behind her ear as she studied Isaac. The little boy was loving the attention.

"Hey, man," he said as he walked up to Isaac and picked him up. Isaac squealed and wiggled.

"Let me go, Uncle Steppen," he shouted.

"You can't run off on me like that." Stephen found Isaac's armpit and started tickling.

"We were having a lovely conversation," Holly said as she peered up at him.

Stephen met her gaze. "Oh really? About what?"

Holly stood, putting herself within inches of him. Out of instinct, Stephen took a step back.

"He said something about me being the Grinch's sister?" Holly folded her arms.

Stephen swallowed and glanced down at Isaac, who was completely distracted with trying to tickle Stephen. Stephen wrapped his arms around Isaac, trapping the boy's arms and holding him still. "Oh he did, did he?" Stephen laughed, hoping to dissuade Holly. "Well, kids do say the darnedest things, huh?"

Holly raised her eyebrows as she drummed her fingers on her arm. "They sure do. Especially when they hear it from adults."

Not sure what to say, he just shrugged. "We really should get going. Isaac and I have lots to do."

Isaac had given up trying to wiggle out of his grip and glanced over at Holly. "You should come with us. We're decorating the trees for Santa."

"Oh, she doesn't want to," Stephen said. "She's too busy."

Holly narrowed her eyes as she glanced between Stephen and Isaac.

"Please?" Isaac asked. "It'll be so much fun. I'm the best decorator in the whole world."

Stephen glanced down to see Isaac nodding like what he said was the truth. Man, he loved this kid. "It's true. He is the best."

Holly's jaw dropped, and she placed her hands on her hips. "No way. You took that title from me?"

"What?" Isaac asked, his eyes wide. "You were the best?"

Holly pushed her hair back and nodded. "Of course. The absolute best."

Isaac began to jump up and down. "Does that mean you'll help us?"

Holly glanced up at Stephen. He shrugged, hoping that she felt no pressure from him. Then she dropped her gaze back down to Isaac and nodded. "I guess I could help out."

Isaac whooped and sprinted toward the kitchen. Not knowing

where his nephew was going or what he was planning to do, Stephen took off after him. He could feel Holly keeping pace with him.

He glanced over his shoulder. "What happened to no decorations?" he asked as he pushed through the kitchen's swinging door —holding it open as she came up behind him.

Holly paused and met his gaze. Then she shrugged. "I figured it couldn't hurt. Plus, he's a cute kid. He deserves a great Christmas." She headed for the outside door, which had been left wide open— no doubt by Isaac. She slipped on her shoes and disappeared outside.

Stephen stood there, shocked that she'd actually said that. For a moment, he'd caught a glimpse of the girl he once knew. Her smile. Her spontaneous personality. And she liked his nephew—it was too much.

He growled as he pushed down his emotions and stomped over to the door. He needed to knock it off. She wasn't there to rekindle anything. She was there to take away the only thing that had ever stuck around for him. Christmas Inn. He couldn't forget that.

By the time he got to the garage, Holly and Isaac had pulled down most of the Christmas decorations. They were laughing as Isaac twirled himself up in the tinsel.

Holly was sitting on one of the bins as she listened to Isaac rattle off everything he wanted from Santa. She seemed so at ease, sitting there, nodding at every item.

It almost made Stephen want to pick up Isaac and run away. He wanted to declare that Christmas was over—they weren't going to fake happiness when the inn was going to be sold so soon after the holidays.

But, he couldn't crush his nephew like that, so he just moved over to stack three bins on top of each other and then hoist them up. "Come on, the trees aren't going to decorate themselves," he said as he made his way to the garage door and out into the cold.

In the time it took Holly and Isaac to drag two bins into the house, Stephen carried in the remainder. There was something soothing about having a job to do. One that worked his muscles and let him release some of his pent-up frustration.

Just as he set the last bin down, he glanced up to see that Holly and Isaac had already opened one and were pulling out the lights.

"Which one do you want to decorate first?" Holly asked as she pointed to the trees in the foyer, by the reception desk, and in the living room.

Isaac tapped his chin before he pointed to the one in the living room. Stephen had chopped down the twelve-footer himself. He'd started a Christmas tree farm years ago and had been saving this baby for a special occasion.

Since he wasn't going to see another Christmas at the inn, it felt like the perfect time to cut it down. But he wasn't sure he wanted Holly to decorate it. Though there was no way of saying that without sounding like a jerk.

He tried to remind himself that this was for Isaac, so if that was the tree he wanted to decorate, Stephen was going to do it with him.

"Come on, I'll lift you up so you can string the top," Stephen said as he hoisted Isaac onto his shoulders and bumped him up and down as he walked over to the tree. Isaac laughed as he clung to Stephen's head.

Holly followed after them with the lights in hand.

Isaac started at the top, stringing lights on the branches. Every so often, he'd tell Stephen to spin, which meant for him to move around the tree.

By the time the lights were on, Stephen was dizzy. He lowered Isaac to the ground, and the boy rushed over to Holly. Stephen plopped down on the couch and stretched out his legs as he watched his nephew and Holly continue decorating.

Holly was pulling ornaments from the box and telling Isaac little stories about them. He would, in turn, bounce up and down on the balls of his feet until she handed them over. Then he would cradle the ornaments in his hands as he half walked, half ran over to the tree to find the perfect spot.

Then they would start all over again.

The bottom half of the tree began to rapidly fill up since it was the only spot that Isaac could reach. It was almost mesmerizing to watch Holly and Isaac as they worked. The sight caused a warm feeling to rise up inside of Stephen.

It was a feeling that he fought and welcomed at the same time. It was hard, knowing what Holly was here to do, to see how at peace and at home she was here at Christmas Inn.

Stephen wanted nothing more than to see her smile. To hear her laugh. To open his heart to her like he once had. But she didn't want that. All she wanted was to turn his life upside down.

What was he supposed to do? How was he supposed to fight the feelings that were resurfacing?

He sighed and rubbed his palms on his thighs.

He was an idiot for freaking out like this. He needed to get his head on straight and focus. Holly was here. She was being nice to Isaac. But that didn't mean she was what he needed.

It didn't matter how much he wanted the Holly that he'd known and loved to return, she didn't exist anymore.

And she had a boyfriend, for Pete's sake. Even if she wasn't trying to destroy his life, she still wasn't his for the taking.

Enough frustration had boiled up inside of him that Stephen stood and wandered over to the tree. He was angry now. Why hadn't she said anything to him about this mysterious boyfriend? Why had she allowed him to think she was available?

It wasn't fair—even if he knew, deep down, that it wasn't her job to confess every part of her life to him. He'd lost that right a long time ago. When she broke his heart and left him in Ivy Springs, alone.

"It's looking good, man," Stephen said as he reached out and tousled Isaac's hair.

Isaac bobbed his head up and down as he smiled up at Stephen. "I know." He paused for a split second and then sprinted over to the tree to hang another ornament.

Holly's soft laugh caused Stephen to glance over at her. She looked so calm. So at peace. It physically hurt to look at her. To see her standing there and not be able to do anything about it. He couldn't touch her. Nothing.

"What?" he asked, hoping to distract himself from the utter perfection that was Holly. He rifled around in the bin in front of her and pulled out an ornament just to keep himself busy.

Holly glanced over at him and then back to Isaac. "I just forgot how much I loved decorating trees. I guess, when you don't do it for a long time, it's easy to forget."

"You don't decorate your tree in New York?" Stephen furrowed his brow as he twirled the ornament's string around his finger.

Holly chuckled. "No. Life's too busy. Plus, Christmas wasn't something that I wanted to remember." A cloud hung over her words as she dipped her gaze down to study the floor.

Stephen watched her. He understood the pain she felt. He just wished there was some way he could help her move on. Then, before he knew what he was doing, he reached out and rested his hand on hers.

"Hope loved you," he said. The depth of his voice matched the depth of his feelings. He hated that she was hanging onto this pain.

Holly's gaze moved to his hand then up his arm and settled on his face. He could see the tears that were forming in her eyes as she chewed her bottom lip.

"How do I forgive her?" she whispered.

Stephen studied her. He wasn't sure if that question was for him or for herself.

"Did you read her letters?" he asked.

Holly closed her eyes for a moment. "I don't know how."

"Ornament," Isaac declared as his little hand jutted into their view.

Holly blinked a few times, swiped at her cheeks, and then glanced down at Isaac. "Of course," she said as she handed him another one.

When Isaac headed back to the tree, Stephen studied her, wondering if they were going to pick up from where they had left off.

But Holly kept avoiding his gaze—the moment had passed. Holly was building the wall back up around her heart—and if he was smart, he would be doing the same.

Shoving his hands into his front pockets, he took a step back. As if distancing himself physically meant he could do it emotionally. He studied her for a moment and then blew out his breath.

"What does your boyfriend think of your lack of Christmas spirit?" he asked. Then he winced. He'd wanted it to come out more relaxed...but it just sounded petty and childish.

Holly paused before she turned to him. "He's okay with it. Neither of us is really interested in all the holiday stuff." She handed Isaac another ornament as he raced up to her.

Once he was gone, she didn't turn to look at Stephen. Instead, she moved to lift another bin and set it on the coffee table next to the empty one.

"Stephen?" Blossom's voice came from behind him.

He turned to see her at the reception desk with the phone in hand.

"Yeah?" he asked. He glanced back at Holly, who looked as if she were making a point not to look at him.

"Room seven has a leaky faucet. Do you think you could look at it?"

Not wanting to take his gaze off of Holly, he just said, "Yep."

He wanted Holly to look at him. He wanted to know that she was happy. That her New York life somehow made her happier than she was here. But, as much as she wanted to lie and tell him that Christmas Inn meant nothing to her, he could tell that wasn't true.

Suddenly, he had a mission. Instead of trying to get her to leave, he was going to do everything to remind her of why she wanted to stay. Why Christmas Inn, no matter how much she wanted to fight it, was a part of her.

And he wasn't going to allow her to ignore it anymore.

11

HOLLY

Holly sat in her room later that evening with a mug of hot tea clutched between her hands. Her knees were drawn up in front of her and she was in her flannel pajamas. There was something so comforting about sitting in a bed with pillows surrounding her and drinking tea.

An audiobook played from her phone, which was sitting on the nightstand next to her. The narrator's voice was deep and throaty. It added the perfect ambiance to the mystery that was unfolding.

She set the mug on the nightstand and sighed as she stretched out her legs. Her gaze drifted over to the Christmas trees that were still set up in her room. At first, they had been a nuisance. But she would miss their aroma and the shape of them if they were taken out now. They made her think back to her afternoon spent decorating with Isaac.

Reaching over, she paused the book. Her thoughts were wandering too much, and she was missing snippets of the story. It was probably better to take a break anyway.

Just as she settled back onto the bed, there was a knock at her door. Confused, she pulled the covers off and crossed the room. She peeked out the peephole and her breath caught in her throat.

Stephen was standing out in the hallway. He had on his coat and hat and was busy staring down the hallway at something.

It was annoying, the way her body reacted. Her heart pounded and her stomach twisted as she took in the sight of him. She'd almost broken down in front of him today—and he knew about Tyler. Everything had her thoughts in a whirlwind.

She took a deep breath as she stilled her mind and pulled open the door. When his gaze met hers, her heart pounded so hard that she was pretty sure he could hear it. And then he dropped his gaze to her body and slowly moved it back up, his smile deepening with each inch he covered.

"Comfy?" he asked. The amused hint to his voice made her cheeks warm even more.

"I finished all the work I needed to do today, so I'm taking some me time." She hoped she came across more confident than she felt.

Stephen chuckled as he tossed her a jacket. "Well, get dressed. We're going out. I'll meet you downstairs."

Holly sputtered as she watched him turn and head toward the stairs. "Wait!" she called.

Stephen stopped and turned. "Yeah?"

Her knees weakened from the depth of his gaze. She hated that she was reacting to him this way. It wasn't helping her at all. Falling for Stephen again would only end in heartache.

"Where are we going?" she asked, finally finding the words. It was amazing how he could make her forget how do the simplest things, like speak.

Stephen held her gaze for a moment before his cocky smile returned. "You'll just have to come and find out." With that, he winked and disappeared down the stairs.

Holly blinked a few times, trying to still her heart. Then she took a deep breath as she shut the door.

"I'm selling the inn. I'm selling the inn," she repeated to herself as she hurried over to the armoire that she'd stashed her clothing in.

Fifteen minutes later, with most of her clothing in a pile on the bed, Holly collapsed and blew out a breath. This outing clearly meant way too much to her.

She covered her face with her arm as she closed her eyes. Maybe it was just a momentary lapse in judgement. Maybe, if she just wished hard enough, the stony exterior that she'd worked so hard to build up around her heart would harden again.

She needed to talk to Talia. Her best friend had a way of helping her see sense.

She groaned as she reached for the nightstand. After locating her phone, she pulled up Talia's number. A few seconds later, ringing filled the air as video chat attempted to connect.

Talia's face filled the screen. Thumping music could be heard in the background while strobing lights made the screen flash. Talia's smile was wide. "Holly!"

Holly furrowed her brow. "Where are you?"

Talia moved the phone around to show the club she was in. "Hanging with my family," she said as she panned across the people sitting at the table with her.

Holly blinked a few times. "You're at a club? With your family?"

Talia laughed. The background shifting as she stood up and started walking. "My baby brother is a DJ. We're here to support him." And then she started dancing with some random guy. "And get my groove on." She laughed.

Holly smiled and rolled her eyes. "I love your family," she said.

Talia turned away for a moment and spoke with someone that Holly couldn't see. "I'll be right back," she said.

A muffled voice responded, and a few seconds later, the noise died down and everything around Talia went dark. "Okay. I'm outside," she said. "What's up?"

Feeling bad that she was pulling her friend away from her family, Holly began to shake her head. "Why did you answer when you're with your family?"

Talia shrugged. "You are my family," she said, matter-of-factly.

Holly smiled. "Ah, you're so sweet."

Talia rolled her eyes. "If that's all you wanted to talk about, then I'll head back inside."

Holly laughed as she sat up. "Okay, okay, that's not why I called."

Talia looked expectantly into the phone. "All right then. Why did you call?"

Suddenly, Holly didn't know what she was going to say. Voicing the feelings that were rolling around inside of her felt wrong. Once she let them out, there was no way she was going to be able to stick them back in. If she shared them, they would be real. And she wasn't sure she was ready for that.

Scratch that. She was definitely not ready for them to be real.

So she gave Talia a sheepish look as she shrugged. "I was just wondering how you were doing."

Talia looked less than thrilled. "I know when you're lying, Holly." She furrowed her brows. "What's going on in Massachusetts?"

Holly studied her friend's earnest expression and sighed, not wanting to keep things bottled up inside anymore.

"Nothing," she said. "Stephen asked me to go somewhere with him tonight, and…I can't figure out what to wear." She closed her eyes, feeling like an idiot.

Talia raised her eyebrows. "Is this a *good* can't figure out or a *bad* can't figure out."

Holly blew out her breath. "It's an 'I have no idea and I'm about to puke' figure out."

"Show me your options," Talia said, her voice taking on a commanding tone.

"You're amazing," Holly said.

Talia snorted. "Tell me something I don't already know."

Holly rested her phone against the lamp on the dresser and proceeded to work through the items of clothing she'd brought. Talia voiced her opinion about all of them until they finally settled on a pair of black jeans with a pink flannel button-up shirt. Talia instead that Holly wear her hair down and put on some makeup. Then Talia's mom appeared, telling Talia that she was missing the whole performance.

Holly told her that she could take it from there and they said goodbye.

Holly's screen went black as silence filled the room. She was standing in front of the mirror, staring at herself. What was she doing? Why did she care this much?

Letting out a frustrated growl, she stuffed her phone into her back pocket and turned, pushing her hair from her face. She was being an idiot, getting all worked up over nothing. She needed to stop overanalyzing things and focus.

The feelings that were creeping up on her were because she had a history with Stephen. That was all. She loved Tyler. She was with Tyler. That was what she needed to remember.

"I'm with Tyler and I'm selling Christmas Inn," she said to her reflection, hoping that if she spoke the words out loud, it would make her feel stronger, more certain.

She narrowed her eyes as she stared at herself. Her mantra wasn't making her feel any better. If anything, it only allowed the little voice in the back of her mind to respond, *"Ha ha, yeah right."*

Glancing over at the clock, she realized that twenty minutes had passed, so she grabbed her jacket and shoes and headed out into the hallway and down the stairs.

Stephen wasn't in the dining room or living room. Just as she pushed open the kitchen's swinging door, she heard the steady cadence of Stephen's voice. He was sitting on one of the stools next to the counter. In front of him was a tray of freshly baked cookies.

He looked so at home. So at ease that it made Holly's heart hurt. Which frustrated her. What was she doing? Why was she allowing herself to go down this road? Did she really think she would be able to resist him?

History had taught her that, when it came to Stephen, she couldn't resist. Not in the least.

"Hey, come on in," Mrs. Brondy said, startling Holly. She stepped away from the oven and waved Holly over. "We've been waiting for you."

From the corner of her eye, Holly saw Stephen turn. He rested his elbow on the counter and surveyed her. His lips tipped upwards, causing heat to permeate her cheeks. Not wanting to just stand there, she nodded as she marched into the room.

"Sorry it took me so long. I, um…" What was she supposed to say? That she had a clothing dilemma and needed her assistant's help?

Stephen and Mrs. Brondy looked expectant as they waited for her to finish.

"I had a panicked phone call from my assistant, so I needed to help her sort things out."

Stephen nodded as he bit into a cookie and chewed thoughtfully. "You ready now? Everything good?" he asked, slipping off the stool and standing.

Holly hated how her heart picked up speed as he neared. It made her feel like a teenager again, assessing his every movement for hidden meaning.

She was in so much trouble.

He glanced down at her and furrowed his brow as he stared at her. "You okay?

She pinched her lips together and nodded. Thankfully, Stephen dropped it as he nodded to Mrs. Brondy and then held his hand inches from Holly's lower back. "Let's get going, then," he said.

A feeling of desperation rushed over her as she dipped her

head and moved toward the back door. Just as she reached out to grasp the door handle, her fingers brushed Stephen's.

She stifled a gasp as she glanced up to see him staring down at her. Holly's mind swam from the smell of his cologne and how close his body was to hers. It was intoxicating, standing there next to him.

Gathering her courage, she stepped out onto the porch, pulling her jacket in close around her. The cold wind hit her face, causing her to hunch her shoulders and bring the collar of her coat closer to her cheeks.

She waited for Stephen to shut the door. She watched as he squinted, his gaze traveling beyond the porch.

"Where are we headed?" she asked. Her voice was surprisingly calm. With the way her stomach was twisting and turning, she half-expected to sound just as discombobulated as she felt.

Stephen glanced down at her as a smile crept across his lips. He pulled his collar up and shrugged. "That is a secret." Then he turned and descended the porch steps. He took a few steps forward before turning back to her. "Coming?"

If she was being completely honest, she wasn't sure she could mentally handle taking a trip with Stephen. She wrapped her arms around her chest to ward off her unease—and the freezing cold.

She allowed her mind to settle before she took a deep breath and nodded. She was a *tad* interested in seeing what Stephen had planned for the two of them.

Stephen was the king of grand gestures. It was one thing she'd always loved about him and secretly wished Tyler did more. Stephen had a way of making her feel special. Like no one else in the entire world mattered.

And for this one night, for this freezing cold and intensely magical Christmas, she was going to allow herself to feel how she'd always felt when wrapped in Stephen's presence.

Safe. Protected. And cherished.

Tomorrow morning, when she woke up, she would go back to reality. Back to what she'd come here to do. She'd get the inn ready to sell so she could get back to her life in New York.

But right then, she was going to grab the present by the horns and let it lead her where it may.

After all, what did she have to lose?

12

STEPHEN

Stephen slowed his gait, waiting to hear if Holly was following after him. He wanted to turn around, to look, but he feared how he would feel if she wasn't coming. Had this been a mistake? Should he have left things where they were with Holly?

Did he honestly think some sleigh ride through the woods and hot chocolate at Christmas Town would change her mind? Was he really that naive?

Of all the things he remembered Holly being, easy to persuade wasn't one of them. When she got an idea in her head, she did it. And when she decided that she wasn't going to do something, it was like pulling teeth to convince her otherwise.

Then, from the corner of his eye, he caught sight of movement. His heart picked up speed as he turned to see Holly fall into step with him.

"This better not be the summer of freshman year all over again," she said as she tucked her face lower into her jacket.

Stephen couldn't hide his smile as he cleared his throat. "I can't believe you remember that."

"You led me into the woods for some secret picnic that was set up on top of a red ant hill. I got bit all over." She shot him a less than enthused look. "That kind of thing is hard to forget."

Stephen chuckled as he led her toward the stables, where he'd hitched the horses to the carriage. It was nice, reminiscing with her about the past. Perhaps, even with what had happened between Holly and her grandmother, her good memories would be just what she needed to move on.

And that gave him hope. More hope than he'd felt in a long time.

Not wanting these new feelings to grow too big, he cleared his throat and glanced down at Holly. "Thanks," he said as he guided her toward the stable door.

Holly obliged and a few seconds later asked, "For what?"

Stephen pulled open the door and held it as he waited for Holly. She took a few steps but then paused, glancing up at him. His heart began to pound in his chest as he took in her bright blue eyes and soft, pale skin. Her dark hair accentuated the curves of her face, bringing to the surface so many memories that it made his body ache.

Ache to touch her. Ache to be closer to her.

He needed something to distract himself. If not, he feared what he would do. Reaching out for Holly was the last thing he should do, and yet, it was the only thought floating around in his mind.

"For coming with me," he said, his voice deepening with emotion. He cleared his throat. "For trusting me."

Holly's eyes widened. He felt open and vulnerable, like he had the night she left. When he'd confessed his feelings to her but she'd misread everything. She'd taken his words as him siding with her grandmother. They'd fought—and he regretted that with every fiber of his being. But when he'd gone back the next day, Holly had been determined to leave. Her bags were packed and there wasn't anything he could say to convince her to stay.

And that had been that. It was the last time he'd spoken to Holly.

It amazed him how quickly his mind and body remembered how to love her. Like riding a bicycle, it was engrained in his mind.

Like breathing, his body just did it.

The silence that settled around them felt deafening. Her gaze held his for a moment before she sighed and ducked into the stable. "Of course. It's just for one night," she said as she wrapped her arms around herself.

He studied her, wondering if she meant what she said. And then he felt like an idiot. Of course she meant what she said. He was the only one between the two of them who was acting like an idiot.

She'd made it perfectly clear when she walked into Christmas Inn that she intended to sell the place. He was the one who was holding onto the hope that he could change her mind.

Clearing his throat—and his mind—he focused on what he was doing. He was trying to remind Holly what Christmas meant to her, not fall in love with her all over again.

As much as it hurt to admit, he knew that asking her not to sell Christmas Inn for his sake was a fool's errand. But, if he could somehow appeal to her Christmas spirit, maybe she would change her mind for herself.

So she needed to be reminded of the meaning of the holiday season, and that was what he was going to do.

"Come on," he said as he passed by her. He waved toward the carriage, and Holly's eyes widened.

"When did you guys get this?" she asked, her voice reverent. She reached out to touch the mahogany wood that had been intricately carved with small Christmas scenes.

Stephen laughed. He understood her reaction. It was the same one he had when he'd picked it up. "I got in in Albany last year. There's a man there who carves them by hand. It was expensive but worth it." He moved over to the horses who were shifting their weight. He pulled on the straps to make sure everything was secure.

Holly was still standing to the side, running her gaze over the carriage. Once Stephen verified that everything was secure, he walked over to her and nodded at the seat. Blankets were folded and set on the floor of the carriage.

Holly glanced over at him with her eyes wide. "We're going in this?"

Stephen nodded. "That was the plan." Then he furrowed his brow. "Unless you don't want to."

Holly shook her head. "No, I want to." She climbed up the stairs and situated herself on the far end of the bench.

Stephen scanned the horses one more time before he grabbed both sides of the carriage and pulled himself up. Once he was situated, he reached down to grab a blanket and then shook it out.

"For you," he said as he laid it on Holly's lap.

She nodded, reaching out to adjust the blanket. Just as she did, her fingers brushed his. Even though they both wore gloves, a jolt of electricity rushed through Stephen. He couldn't help but glance down at her.

Did she feel it too?

If she did, she didn't acknowledge it. She continued adjusting the blanket and tucking it in around her legs. Needing something to do, Stephen grabbed another blanket and handed it to her. Then he sat back and grabbed the reins. He needed to focus on driving the carriage and not be distracted by the feelings that were becoming harder and harder to ignore.

"You don't want one?" Holly asked. He looked at her, and she nodded toward the last blanket. He shook his head.

"I'm good." Then he clicked his tongue and shook the reins. The horses began to walk. He guided them out of the stable and into the crisp night air.

As they progressed down the driveway and out onto the main

road, Stephen found himself relaxing. The trees that lined the road rose high above them. The dark branches contrasted against the pure white snow. There wasn't a cloud in the sky, and the stars sparkled above them.

The full moon lit the road in front of them. Reaching over, Stephen turned on some instrumental Christmas music on his phone and allowed the soft sound to wash over him. His nerves relaxed as he settled back on the bench.

"It's beautiful," Holly whispered.

He tipped his head slightly so he could peek over at her. She had her head back, exposing her long neck and creamy white skin. His own body heated at the memory of touching her.

Frustrated, he turned his attention back to the road, determined to keep his eyes on it. Helping Holly remember Christmas didn't involve him falling for her again.

The music floated around them as they fell into silence. He could sense Holly next to him as she began to relax. It made him smile. His plan was working.

"Why are you smiling?" Holly asked.

Stephen turned to study her for a moment before he shrugged. "You're relaxing."

She glanced around. "I am? How can you tell?"

Stephen chuckled as he reached into the basket behind him where he'd stashed dinner and a few thermoses of hot chocolate. After locating one, he handed it to Holly. "Here, open this."

She took it and turned it over in her hands. "What is it?"

Stephen dove back into the basket and located the two mugs. He handed them to Holly. "What else?" he asked as he returned to holding the reins.

Holly was quiet and then she laughed. It was soft and melodious. "I can't believe you made it." She twisted the thermos lid and inhaled. "The ultimate hot chocolate," she said, her voice reverent.

"Of course I made it. I make it every year." Once, when Holly was sick, Stephen had snuck her a mug of hot chocolate behind

Hope's back. Holly had been upset that she was missing Christmas, so Stephen stuck every piece of Christmas candy into the drink. It was his way of helping her feel included.

The candies had turned into a blob at the bottom of the mug and made her sicker, but the tradition was born. The ultimate hot chocolate.

Holly laughed. "I haven't had it since I...left." Her voice trailed off as the meaning of her words hung heavy in the air.

Stephen's smile died as he continued to stare down the road. It was amazing how, one second, he was flying high, connecting with Holly like he'd once done. And then reality smacked him back down to Earth. Back to his life and the painful memories that existed there.

If only things were different. If only Holly had never left. He was pretty sure his future would look a lot different than it did.

The sound of metal clinking against porcelain drew his attention. Holly was pouring the hot chocolate into a mug. Once it was full, she passed it over to him.

"Thanks for thinking of me," she said softly as she glanced first at the mug and then back to Stephen.

He studied her for a moment and then took the mug from her. "Of course," he said. Two words that emerged with so much meaning that they tugged at his heart strings.

Did she seriously think that he would forget about her? That he'd somehow stopped thinking about her in the years she'd been gone? She was fool to think that he would forget her. He doubted he ever could.

Needing to distract himself, he focused on the road and sipped the hot chocolate. He was worried that he'd confess the feelings that were coursing through him. And if he did, he wouldn't be able to take it back.

He'd already been rejected by Holly once, he wasn't too keen on having it happen again.

"Oh, gosh," Holly said as she pulled the mug from her lips. She coughed a few times, covering her lips with her fingers. "Was it always this sweet?"

Stephen laughed as he nodded. "Yeah. It's basically inedible, but you get used to it."

Holly laughed. She studied the mixture again and then shrugged and took another sip. Her face contorted into a look of disgust as she swallowed. Even when her face was scrunched up, she still looked adorable.

She licked her lips and then glanced over at him. "What?" she asked. "Is there something on my face?"

Realizing that he was staring at her, Stephen turned back to the road. "Nope," he said as he took another drink.

"Oh."

"There's hot cider in the other thermos if you want," he said as he tipped his head toward the basket behind him.

"Really? You don't mind?" she asked.

Stephen furrowed his brow. "Why would I mind?"

Holly shrugged as she held her mug with both hands. "You made this for me."

Stephen's jaw dropped. He hoped she wouldn't see that she had hit the nail on the head. He'd made it to help her remember the good memories at Christmas Inn.

"I make it every year, remember. You were just lucky enough to be here when I made this year's batch." He chuckled and took another sip. "This is Ivy Springs goodness right here," he said as he held up his mug. "I don't know what they are serving you in New York, but your taste buds have changed."

From the corner of his eye, he saw Holly toss the contents of her mug over the side. He glanced over at her with an exaggeratedly shocked expression.

She shrugged as she twisted around and began digging in the basket behind them. "I'm so sorry, I just can't." She held up the thermos of cider triumphantly. "If I drink any more of that, I'll be sick."

She settled back onto her seat and unscrewed the thermos's lid. After she filled her mug, she sighed as she cuddled under the blankets. "Perfect," she whispered.

The tone of her voice sent shivers of pleasure across Stephen's body. Those feelings made him uncomfortable, so he shifted in his seat, hoping he could focus on what he was doing there.

"I bet they don't have this in New York," he said as he motioned toward the woods around them.

Holly followed his gesture with her gaze and then shrugged. "You can actually get horse drawn carriage rides everywhere. In fact"—she paused to take another drink—"they have people who will bike you places."

Stephen glanced over at her. His plan to make her see the charm of Ivy Springs didn't seem to be working. "Really?" he asked.

She pinched her lips together as she turned and nodded. But then she sighed. "But it's nothing like Ivy Springs. Everywhere you go there are buildings. And it smells. No one takes time to just stop and enjoy. You're always rushing, rushing, rushing." Her voice faded off as she got lost in her thoughts.

"Then why do you live there?" Stephen asked.

When she didn't answer right away, he glanced over, hoping he hadn't overstepped. She was staring into her mug.

"It's not that easy, giving everything up and moving somewhere else. I guess I wanted to put down roots for myself." Her voice grew so quiet that Stephen had to lean in. "Make a place where I would feel safe. Where no one could hurt me."

Stephen leaned back so he could study her. The proud, hard exterior that she'd been sporting this entire trip was crumbling. She was letting him in, and that thought made his heart swell.

"Holly—"

"Don't," she said.

He stared at her, but she kept her gaze down. Her shoulders

were tight, and he could tell that there was a war raging inside of her. One that she didn't know how to win.

And even though he wanted to help her, to fix the pain that she was feeling inside, he couldn't. She would never be truly happy if she was forced to do anything.

Hope had already made so many decisions for her, because she thought she knew what was best for Holly. And even though he felt the same, he knew he needed to back off.

If he loved Holly—and every minute he was with her made it harder to deny—he'd let her take the time she needed to figure things out for herself. Wounds of the heart took longer to heal than physical hurts. And when she was ready to move forward, he'd be there to help her.

Turning his gaze back to the road, he nodded. "Of course."

He hoped she knew that when he uttered those two words, those two simple words, he was really trying to say *I love you.*

HOLLY

Holly hated what she was doing to Stephen. She really did. She knew what he was trying to do, and, honestly, it was working.

He was hoping that if Holly remembered all the good things about Ivy Springs, then she might rethink selling Christmas Inn. That if she could learn to love the place that had given her so much pain, she would change her plans.

Stephen wasn't dumb. He knew her inside and out, and he was charming her. An evening carriage ride? The ultimate hot chocolate? (Even though it was way worse than she remembered.) Everything he was doing was calculated. He was drawing on her memories to help her see what she would be abandoning if she sold her childhood home.

But he didn't care about her. He cared about the inn. If he really cared about her, he wouldn't ask her to keep the inn. He would know the weight she carried and what facing the pain of her past might do to her.

Being back at Christmas Inn made her feel as if she would crumble. She was holding tight to her pain, because if she didn't have that, then who was she? How would she go back to her life in New York? How could anything be the same anymore?

Why did things have to change?

Closing her eyes, she tipped her head back and took in slow, steady breaths. She didn't want to break down. Not right then. Not in front of Stephen. He would sense her weakness and he would use it against her.

If she was so unhappy with her life, how would selling Christmas Inn help her? She could already hear his argument.

And she didn't have an answer to that. She didn't need to know how everything was going to turn out. She didn't need anyone but herself. If she didn't allow others into her life, she could never get hurt. Which was why Tyler was perfect for her. He had his own life and aspirations, and she had hers. And it wasn't until that moment that she realized how distant they really were.

"Are you okay?" Stephen's voice cut through her thoughts.

She straightened and glanced over at him to see his worried gaze. Realizing that she probably looked as if she were having a mental breakdown, Holly nodded and pushed herself up on the bench. "Yes, of course," she said as she dabbed at her eyes.

Stephen furrowed his brow and then sighed. "Listen, I know what you're thinking."

Holly scoffed. Did he really? He couldn't possibly know what she was going through.

Stephen stared at her. "You're hurt. You feel betrayed. You feel as if the whole world is on your shoulders. And no matter what you do, time marches on. You're not ready, but the present becomes the past, and suddenly, you're stuck holding onto pain while the rest of the world has moved on." Stephen had stopped the carriage in a small clearing.

At some point, he must have veered off the road and into the woods. Trees surrounded them on all sides. The trees glistened with string lights, and they lit up the snow in a way that Holly had never seen.

It was like a scene from a movie. Her breath caught in her throat as she glanced around. "Stephen," she whispered. "When did you do this?"

Stephen was watching her with a pained expression on his face, and then he sighed. "Earlier today. When I was avoiding the inn." He jumped down from the carriage. "Don't worry, I didn't just do all this for you. We had Isaac's birthday party out here in August—I strung the lights then. I just brought out the generator to run the lights." He held out his hand to help her climb down.

Her brain told her not to take his hand, that touching Stephen was the last thing she should do, but her heart won out. She didn't want to hurt his feelings.

As she placed her hand in his, his jaw tightened for a moment, and she wondered what that meant. Was this just as hard for him as it was for her?

Her heart pounded in her chest as she let him guide her down to the ground. Silence engulfed them as they stood next to each other in the quiet clearing.

Stephen cleared his throat and dropped her hand. He glanced over at her and gave her a forced smile. Then he nodded toward the back of the carriage. "I'll get the food," he said.

Not sure what her voice would sound like, Holly just nodded.

Stephen turned to grab the basket. Ready to get some distance, Holly walked over to the horses. They were shifting their weight as they stood in their traces.

Holly approached them from the front. She reached out her hand, and one of the horses nuzzled her with his nose. She laughed as she leaned in and tipped her face towards his.

"You're simple to love," she whispered.

The horse moved his head, and Holly decided that meant he was agreeing with her. She pulled back and rubbed his nose with her hand. It was easy, standing here, loving the horse.

But that confusing man who was unloading a basket of food from the carriage? She couldn't wrap her head around how she felt about him.

Why would he want to be stuck in a small town like Ivy Springs as the caretaker of Christmas Inn. It didn't really speak to the adventurous boy she remembered.

He'd always said he would leave Ivy Springs and make something of himself. And yet, here he was, stuck in the one place they'd both dreamed of leaving.

He must have sensed her staring at him because after he set the basket down on the picnic table, he turned and met her gaze. Her cheeks flushed, but she didn't glance away. Instead, she furrowed her brow. It was strange, but she wanted him to know that she was thinking about him.

She'd spent so much time trying to forget him. Forget the inn. But now that she was faced with Stephen and their past, there was a part of her that wanted to hash it out. To figure out what had gone wrong.

"What?" he asked as he started unpacking. A bottle of wine. Bread. Something in a small Tupperware container.

Holly's stomach growled, so she gave the horse one last pat on the nose and made her way to the table. She saw his shoulders tighten as she neared, and even though she didn't know what that meant, she decided to take it as a good sign.

"I was just thinking..." she said as she climbed up onto the table and sat down. She glanced up at Stephen, who had stopped unpacking and was staring off into the distance.

"Yeah? About what?" he asked. Whatever trance he'd been under, he snapped out of it and continued to remove items from the basket.

When he opened a container full of grapes, Holly reached out and grabbed one. She popped it into her mouth and chewed thoughtfully.

"You," she finally said.

Stephen paused and then looked over at her. "What about me?"

Holly grabbed a cracker and took a bite. "Why did you stay here in Ivy Springs?" She figured she might as well be as forward as possible. There was no need to beat around the bush anymore. She was here. She might as well find out.

Stephen paused and then dipped a cracker in some cheese spread. It looked delicious, so Holly did the same. Stephen swallowed and brushed off his hands as he turned to study her.

"After you left, Hope was distraught. I didn't think she could handle losing me, too. So I stayed, just until she could get her feet under her." His brow furrowed as he watched her.

She knew he was waiting for her reaction. He wasn't mincing words. He was speaking truth and waiting to see if she could handle it. And, sure, it hurt. It caused the weight in her chest to intensify, but she just nodded and held his gaze. She could handle what he had to say.

After all, she'd been the one to ask him. If she didn't want to hear the truth, she should have kept her lips sealed.

Stephen waited a few more seconds before he continued. "I was ready to leave. I had a full-ride scholarship to college. I was going to study engineering." He sighed as he grabbed another cracker. "But then Blossom got into an accident."

A crackling sensation rose in her throat as she listened to his words. He seemed so sad. So broken. She wanted to wrap her arms around him just so he knew he wasn't alone.

She hadn't imagined that her leaving Ivy Springs would do this to him. Sure, he'd made her mad, but breaking things off and leaving him like she had was wrong. He had been left behind, picking up the pieces that she'd left in her wake.

"What happened?" she asked. Call her crazy, but she wanted to know more. She wanted to help carry this weight that he was dragging around with him.

Stephen dropped his gaze, staring a bit too hard at the wooden tabletop in front of him. "She was in a car accident. She was drunk and hit a tree." He swallowed, and she could see the muscles strain in his jaw. The intensity of his voice sent shivers down his back. "She'd tried calling me from the bar to see if I could come pick her up. But I didn't answer. I was studying and didn't want to be bothered." He cleared his throat. "I should have been there for her."

Without thinking, Holly reached out and rested her hand on his. He straightened as if he wasn't sure what to do with her gesture. But Holly didn't move. She was going to show him support and sympathy.

Stephen hesitated and then reached out and rested his other hand on hers. His hands were warm and familiar and sent shivers across her skin. Her breath caught in her throat as he raised his gaze up to meet hers.

He held it for a moment as if he, too, were trying to figure out what any of this meant—if it meant anything.

Holly gave him a small smile. He had to know that she cared about him. He had to know that she would have been there for him had she known. Or, at least, she hoped she would have been.

"Your grandmother let Blossom and Isaac live with me at the inn. She gave Blossom a job, and it took months, but Blossom was finally able to come out of her depression. Realizing that she was never going to be able to walk again, that her life had forever changed, was really hard on her."

Stephen let go of her hands and scrubbed his face as he tipped his head up toward the sky. "That is why I never left. I had people depending on me." When he glanced back down at her, he shrugged. "Sure, it's not as adventurous as I thought my life would be, but I love this place. Plus, Isaac has a way of making every-thing an adventure." His lips tipped up into a small smile at the mention of his nephew.

Holly laughed as Isaac's wide smile and sweet spirit entered her mind. "He's a great kid. He's lucky to have such a good and loyal uncle."

Stephen's smile faded. He looked as if he were chewing on her words. Holly wasn't sure what she was doing, but she couldn't help to allow the feelings she'd always had for Stephen to resurface.

Honestly, they'd never truly left. They were still there, filling her body with warmth and fear. Fear that he would hurt her again. Fear of what loving him might do to her. Fear of what her future looked like if she allowed herself to feel for him.

The meticulously perfect life she'd planned for herself in New York might not be the life she actually wanted. And that thought scared her. Ignoring her past was far easier than facing it.

And yet, here she was, facing a part of her past that she never thought she would have to deal with again.

"You'll find that I'm loyal to a lot of people," he said. His voice was deep, and she could sense his meaning in every syllable.

"Stephen," she whispered. It was hard to believe that even after all of these years, it was so easy to fall into rhythm with Stephen. And in that moment, she realized she wasn't the only one feeling things. From the depth of his stare and the way he leaned in toward her, she could tell he felt things too.

What did that mean for her? For him? What was she supposed to do with that knowledge?

Her heart was pounding. When she glanced up to meet his gaze, she could feel the intensity in his stare. He leaned closer, and she didn't move away. She welcomed his approach and the feeling she got when he was near. There was a part of her that was calling out for his closeness.

Begin near Stephen sent a mixture of excitement and fear coursing through her. Never had she felt so at home and so scared at the same time.

"I wanted you to come back," he whispered as he reached his hand up and cradled her cheek.

His touch was warm and inviting, and she couldn't help but

lean into it. Her heart sang from his touch. It was everything she'd been trying to convince herself she didn't need.

"You did?" she whispered as he leaned closer. She could feel his warmth as he hovered in front of her.

"It may have been one of the reasons I stayed. I wanted to be here when you got back." His gaze dipped down to her lips. Out of instinct, she bit her lower lip. That caused him to glance up and meet her gaze.

Tears filled her eyes as so many emotions coursed through her. She wanted to give in. She wanted to allow herself to love Stephen like she'd done in the past. It was so easy it took no effort at all.

"Stephen..." she whispered, but then she let the sentence die as she fought with what to say next. Nothing felt genuine. It all felt forced. She knew what she *should* say. She knew she should pull away, but it was as if she were rooted to the spot.

And then his lips were on hers. They were soft and gentle and full of so much feeling that it took her breath away.

She wasn't sure what to do. She wanted to respond. She wanted to kiss him back. It felt so right, being there with him. But doubt and regret began to creep into her mind.

She'd already failed at so many things. She'd already made so many wrong decisions, and she didn't want kissing Stephen to fall into that category.

If she was going to kiss him again, it was going to be because it was the right thing to do. Not an emotion-filled mistake. And definitely not when she was still dating Tyler.

So despite the desire she had to lose herself in holding Stephen —in kissing him—she pulled back enough to break their connection.

"I can't," she whispered, unable to look him in the eye. She didn't want to see the disappointment she was sure was resting there.

"Can you take me back to the inn?" she asked. She needed to be alone. She needed to figure out what she was going to do.

Despite the way she felt about Stephen, it didn't change her future plans. She was going to sell the inn and marry Tyler. It was the future she'd planned for herself, and she needed to see it through. She was tired of running when things got hard. If she had truly changed, she needed to start taking her commitments seriously.

Stephen stepped back, and a pained expression passed over his face as he studied her. "Holly, I—"

"I can't, Stephen. I will always love you, but that doesn't change what I need to do." She winced as her words met her ears. It wasn't until she heard them that she realized how harsh it sounded.

Stephen parted his lips. Then he scoffed and glanced around before finally meeting her eye again. "Don't do this," he said.

Holly fought the tears that we're forming on her lids. She'd gone this far, she might as well keep going. "I have to sell the inn. This"—she motioned between the two of them—"doesn't change that."

Stephen took another step back. His expression looked like he'd been slapped. And she hated it.

"You've given up so much of your life to that place," she said. "Selling it could free us both." She climbed off the table and stood next to him. "It's the break you'd never take for yourself."

Why couldn't he see that he was trapped? He'd given so much for everyone else, and she was going to help him let go of the weight around his neck. The inn was crushing him, but he didn't see it.

He stilled as he stared at her. "Staying is a choice I made. No one can take that away from me." He pulled off his hat and pushed his hands through his hair. "And I don't consider taking care of my loved ones a burden that I need a break from." He shoved his hat back on as he continued to stare down at her.

He was hurting and she hated that she was causing it. She

parted her lips to speak, but he just turned his attention to the table and began packing up food.

Not wanting to leave on that note, she stepped forward. "Stephen, I—"

"Please don't," he said, his shoulders rounding as he tipped his head forward. "I already said goodbye to you once. If you're still planning on leaving, don't make me fall for you again."

Holly stared at him, wishing she could change the past. She wished that things were simpler, but they weren't. Matters of the heart never were.

So she remained quiet as she helped him close the containers of food and set them back in the basket.

The ride home was quiet. Stephen sat rigid in his seat with his hands on the reins. He wasted no time climbing down once they got to the stables. He nodded toward the house. "I'll take care of everything. You can head back."

Holly stared at him as he busied himself with undoing the straps around the horses. She hesitated as she thought about speaking. She wanted to explain herself, but she knew he didn't want to hear it.

Instead, she nodded and took off toward the house. Once she was in her room, she collapsed on her bed, burying her face in the comforter.

The evening definitely hadn't gone as planned.

If anything, her whole situation had just got a lot harder. Her mind was swimming with thoughts and questions, none of which she had answers to. She tried to figure out how she was going to survive the next few days at Christmas Inn.

Because, with the way she was feeling, she doubted she'd even be able to do that.

14

STEPHEN

Stephen woke up the next morning in a sour mood. Apparently, hours of sleep weren't going to blot out the fact that Holly had basically pulled his heart from his chest and stomped on it. Repeatedly.

All he could do was retreat to his house and lick his wounds. The drive to get up and be productive had all but disappeared. But the responsibility that bore down on him was hard to ignore. No matter how he was feeling, he couldn't forget what he needed to do.

If this was going to be his last Christmas at the inn, then he needed to push forward and make it the best one ever. Isaac deserved it. The guests deserved it. Even he deserved it.

No longer was he going to waste his breath trying to convince Holly that she wanted to keep this place or that it deserved to stay open. He'd played all his cards, and in so doing, he'd fallen in love with Holly all over again.

So there he was, right back at the starting line with a broken heart and a bruised ego.

Growling with frustration, Stephen pulled his off covers and slipped his feet to the floor. He winced as the cold wood shocked his system and jolted him fully awake.

He stood and stumbled into the shower. Steam filled the bathroom, coating the mirror and surrounding him in warmth. He breathed in the moist air, and it helped calm his nerves.

If he was going to survive a few more days with Holly, he needed to be as zen as possible.

He took his time in the shower, washing his body and allowing the hot water to pound the stress from his muscles. He could have stayed there all day, but he knew he had things to do. Animals to feed and guests to look after.

He couldn't ignore his responsibilities, even if that was the only thing he wanted to do right then. That wasn't who he was, and no old flame was going to change that about him.

He was going to put on a smile—even if it felt fake—and he was going to move on with his life.

He'd sat for so long in the shadows of what they could have been. Of what he'd never fought for. But now he had. He'd told her how he felt. He'd kissed her—but she hadn't kissed him back.

She had given him the closure he needed, now he needed to take that freedom and move forward.

Once he was dried off and dressed, he threw on his jacket and boots and headed out into the crisp morning air. The wind nipped at his ears and neck, causing him to hunch his shoulders to keep the chill from seeping in further.

That morning, he welcomed the cold. He welcomed what the cool air and crisp snow meant. It helped him feel more alive.

He pounded up to the back porch of Christmas Inn, knocking the extra snow from his shoes before heading inside.

The smell of French toast and maple syrup filled his nose as he stepped into the warm kitchen. Mrs. Brondy was standing by the griddle, flipping pieces of French toast. Christmas music carried through the room.

Stephen shut the door behind him—at the behest of Mrs. Brondy—and slipped off his boots. Everything about the scene in front of him was pure perfection. This was what he loved about this time of year and living in a place that celebrated it all year round.

Christmas Inn was a slice of heaven in the frantic, chaotic world. If Holly didn't see that, then he felt sorry for her.

"Good morning," Stephen said as he planted a kiss on Mrs. Brondy's cheek.

She pulled back to stare at him. "Well, you're in a good mood," she said as she grabbed a plate and began dishing him up some food.

Stephen poured himself a cup of coffee as he forced a wide smile. "Of course. Tomorrow is Christmas Eve. Isn't this the time of year we live for?"

Mrs. Brondy handed him a plate full of French toast and eggs. Just as Stephen moved to take it, she paused, not letting go. "Yes, but you're never like this." She narrowed her eyes. "Are you not telling me something?"

Stephen stared at her and then slowly took a sip of his coffee. He wasn't sure exactly what he should say. Last night, Holly made it pretty clear that, no matter what he did, she wasn't going to keep the inn.

The people who worked there deserved to know.

So he took a deep breath and leaned in. "Holly's still moving forward," he said.

Mrs. Brondy raised her eyebrows. "She's selling?" The slouch in her shoulders and disappointment in her voice matched Stephen's mood.

Stephen nodded. "Yep," he said, taking another sip of coffee.

Mrs. Brondy's expression turned nostalgic as she stared off into the distance. Then she sighed and shrugged. "I guess it's my turn to give Holly a letter."

Stephen set his plate down on the counter and ripped off a chunk of toast. He furrowed his brow as he glanced over at her. "Hope gave you a letter, too?"

Mrs. Brondy nodded as she returned to flipping the French toast on the griddle. "It's a Hail Mary. I'm only supposed to whip it out if nothing else worked."

Stephen continued to eat, chewing thoughtfully. Just as he started to pull off another chunk with his fingers, Mrs. Brondy sighed and nodded toward the utensil drawer. "You weren't raised in a barn, Mr. Jones. Eat like a civilized man."

Stephen chuckled as he pulled out a fork. Then he drizzled his toast with syrup and pulled up a barstool next to the counter. The food was warm and delicious and hit the spot just right. "What do you think are in those letters?" he asked through a mouthful of toast and eggs.

Mrs. Brondy shot him an annoyed look as she pressed her forefinger to her lips. "Facts. Feelings. Everything Hope wanted to say to Holly but never got the chance." She sighed as she pressed the back of her wrist to her forehead. "Your perspective changes the older you get. I have a feeling that things that mattered to Hope in the beginning changed toward the end."

Stephen studied Mrs. Brondy. It was strange. Both of them had lived and worked around Hope for so long, and yet, it seemed as if she had known a different Hope than he had.

He took a sip of his coffee to wash down his food, and then he cleared his throat. "What happened? You know, with Holly's mom?"

He'd never asked Hope before. It hadn't felt like his place. Plus, he figured if Hope wanted him to know, she would have told him. But he wished he had. If anything, it would have better equipped him to handle Holly and her issues with Hope.

If he knew what had happened, there just might be a chance that he could help Holly overcome it. Living in a world where she couldn't forgive the people closest to her had to be doing things to

Holly on a spiritual and mental level. And even though he'd decided that he wasn't going to think about Holly—or even care about her—he knew that was impossible.

Holly was always going to be a part of him. And, at least for a few more days, she owned the inn. She was his business until the ink dried on the bill of sale.

Mrs. Brondy sighed as she pulled off the French toast, sprayed down the griddle, and then laid out another batch. She picked up the dish that was now overflowing with food and nodded toward the dining room. "Let me go set these down on the buffet and I'll be right back."

Stephen nodded, grabbing another piece of toast as she walked by. Mrs. Brondy hadn't been gone more than a minute before the kitchen door swung open.

Stephen turned to tease Mrs. Brondy about having superspeed, but instead he was met with Holly's wide eyes. She was dressed in a simple long-sleeve shirt and jeans. She had a mug in her hand, and she stood like a deer in headlights.

Stephen's heart pounded in his chest as he nodded at her and then dropped his gaze down to his plate. There was no way he wanted to have a conversation with Holly.

If she was going to sell the inn, why couldn't she just leave him alone? Why did she have to stick around as a reminder of something he wanted but couldn't have?

"Sorry," she whispered. From the corner of his eye, he saw her enter the kitchen. "They're out of coffee out there," she said as she headed over to the coffee pot.

Stephen shrugged and shoved a forkful of French toast into his mouth. "This is your place. You don't have to tell me what you're doing or why you're doing it."

Holly was halfway through pouring her coffee when she paused and glanced up at him. Her brows were furrowed, and a look of physical pain crossed her face. "Stephen, I—"

"Listen, what happened, happened. Right now, I want to focus on giving the guests here the best Christmas ever. After all, that's why they are here." No longer hungry, he grabbed his dish, dumped the remaining food into the garbage, and set it next to the sink. Then he downed the rest of his coffee—even though it scorched his throat.

He didn't want to stay there in the kitchen any longer.

After setting the mug next to his plate, he turned and glanced over at her. "We're fine," he said as he threw his hands up in surrender.

Holly was just staring at him with her eyes wide and her lips slightly parted. He could tell she was trying to process what he was saying. Trying to find a way to make her decision hurt less.

And that just made him angrier. If she was going to rip his heart out and take away the only thing he'd ever truly loved, then she might as well be confident in her decision. This waffling was killing him. It kept giving him hope that she just might change her mind. Then she would part her lips and confirm what he'd known all along. The Holly he'd grown up with was gone. She'd been replaced by a Christmas-hating, heart-shattering woman.

And nothing was going to change that.

"We'll have a good Christmas, and you'll get your money and get back to the city." He brushed his hands against each other. "Easy peasy."

He tried not to wince as he heard what he'd just said. *Easy peasy?* He'd never said that in his life. How was that proving to Holly that he was okay? Uttering two words that he'd never said in his entire life did not speak to confidence.

If anything, it just showed her exactly what she was doing to him. Just how much she'd broken his heart.

So, before he said anything more idiotic, he strode off into the dining room. He was going to find Isaac and have some fun. They needed to finish the decorations outside and inside, and then he was going to take care of the stables, all while avoiding Holly.

He still had so much to do to get ready for Christmas Eve tomorrow, and wallowing wasn't going to help his workload.

Thankfully, Blossom and Isaac were at their regular table, just finishing up breakfast. Isaac was standing on his chair, bouncing up and down while Blossom tried to convince him to sit down.

A smile spread across his lips as he allowed his affection for his nephew to grow inside of him. This was what Christmas was about, and he was going to share every minute of it with Isaac.

"Hey, man," he said, scooping his nephew up into his arms and spinning him around.

"Don't, he's sticky," Blossom protested.

Stephen glanced at her and shrugged. Then he set Isaac down on the ground and inspected his hands. "Are you sticky?" he asked, noting all the syrup covering his hands.

"I was eating like a monkey," Isaac said, matter-of-factly.

Stephen glanced over at Blossom. "He was eating like a monkey. What do you expect?"

"Ooo eee ooo," Isaac said, imitating a monkey.

Stephen laughed as he raised his hands over his head and did the same. Soon, he was chasing his nephew around the dining room, the both of them chattering like monkeys.

The guests who were finishing up their breakfast stared at them with wide eyes. Stephen just laughed and straightened. "Sorry," he mumbled.

Then he scooped Isaac up and tossed him onto his shoulders. "Come on, sticky monkey, we've got work to do."

Isaac cheered as Stephen carried him over to the bathroom. Just as he passed through the opening that lead into the foyer, Holly stepped out of the kitchen. She met his gaze for a moment.

Stephen kept moving even though he wanted nothing more than to stop and go to her. He hated that Holly was hurting, but there wasn't much he could do about it.

When someone was hell-bent on leaving, there wasn't much anyone could do to stop them. If Holly wanted to go—if that was what was going to make her happy—then he would let her go. He wasn't going to stand in her way.

All he could do now was distract himself. He'd do anything to drown out the ache that was howling inside his chest. Because if he didn't, he wasn't sure he'd survive her leaving.

15

HOLLY

Holly dropped her gaze as Stephen walked out of the dining room. She wasn't sure how she was going to be able to face him after last night. And her interactions with him so far had confirmed her fears.

Leaving Stephen was going to hurt. Again.

Sighing, she held her mug with both hands and made her way back over to her table. The eggs on her plate were cold and her French toast was soggy. None of it seemed very appetizing.

Sighing, she pushed her plate away and leaned back in her chair, sipping her coffee. She stared out the window where the sun was barely peeking through the clouds. Snow was falling, and every so often, the wind would pick it up and swirl it around.

It reminded her of last night, when Stephen took her to that clearing in the woods. Where he'd kissed her.

She hadn't been able to get that memory out of her mind. She fell asleep thinking about it and woke up to the feeling of his lips against hers.

It was like nothing she'd ever experienced. Even when they were kids. This kiss meant something. Something she wasn't willing to acknowledge to herself.

"Are you done with your breakfast?" Blossom asked, pulling Holly from her thoughts.

Holly turned to see Blossom had wheeled up next to her, an expectant look in her eyes.

Not sure what Blossom was getting at, Holly just nodded. "Yes."

Blossom glanced toward the plate and then back to Holly. "Good. Because you're coming with me." Blossom backed up her wheelchair and then began navigating around the tables and pushed-out chairs.

Confused, Holly stared after Stephen's sister, not sure what was happening.

"Come on," Blossom said from over her shoulder.

Holly glanced back at her table and then stood up, deciding it was best to just go along.

She had to hurry to keep up with Blossom, who had passed the reception desk and was making her way toward the back of the inn. Holly pinched her lips as she fought the urge to ask where they were going.

When they got to the end of the hall. Blossom stopped right next to a door. She pulled out a key and stuck it into the lock. Confused, Holly watched. She didn't remember a room being back here.

Blossom pushed a button by the door, and it opened on its own, revealing a small living room. Blossom wheeled inside and then glanced back at Holly. "You can come in," she said.

Holly nodded as she stepped inside. She ran her gaze around. Legos were piled on the coffee table. Toys littered the floor. When she returned her gaze to Blossom, she saw that Blossom was studying her.

"This is where I live," she said.

Holly nodded. "It's nice. I don't remember this being back here."

Blossom sighed as she met Holly's gaze. "It's because your grandmother and Stephen had it built for me after I lost the use of my legs."

Holly pinched her lips as a dull ache rose up inside of her. Confused at what Blossom wanted to her to do with this information, all she could do was nod.

Blossom cleared her throat. "I'm showing you this because I know you've been hurt. I know your grandmother kept information from you." She took a deep breath. "I'm not one to interfere in people's business, but I love your grandmother and I love Stephen. They were both there for me when I was in a really dark place."

She raised her gaze up to Holly's and held it for a moment. "I don't want to see her memory trashed or his heart broken." She eyed Holly. The intensity of her gaze caused Holly to shift.

"Okay," Holly said. She wasn't sure exactly what Blossom was trying to get at. And she wasn't sure she liked the fact that Blossom was inserting herself in Holly's business.

Blossom nodded. "I'm sorry if I'm being too forward, but I've seen the way Stephen looks at you. I want you to realize that if you're leaving at the end of whatever this is, then you need to stay away from him."

Tears pricked Holly's lids. Blossom was right. "I know," Holly whispered.

Blossom studied her and then furrowed her brow. "Look, the three people that I love most in the world love you. You can't be all that bad. I just need you to realize that life is short. One minute, you have everything, then the next? Life changes." She waved toward her legs.

"You can spend so much of your life living in what might have happened instead of enjoying the present." Blossom's voice filled with so much emotion that it took Holly aback. She studied Blossom as she reached up to wipe away a tear.

Holly let Blossom's words sink in around her. There was so much emotion, so much hurt wrapped up in what she'd said, that Holly worried that if she spoke, she would say the wrong thing.

So much of Holly's life was spent living in the past. Her debt. Her relationship with her grandmother. Even her relationship with Tyler. All of it involved a part of herself that she wished she could change. A part of her that she wished she could go back in time and make different.

She'd reacted horribly to what happened with her grandmother. She knew this now. She wished with all of her being that she could go back and make things right. To fix the relationship she regretted giving up from the moment she did it—even if she hadn't been ready to admit it at the time.

The realization of what she'd done and all the time she'd wasted settled around her. Regret filled her chest to the point of bursting. She took in some deep breaths, hoping to calm her nerves.

But no matter how much she tried to control her emotions, tears pricked her eyes and rolled down her cheeks. A soft sob escaped her lips as she glanced around the tiny apartment. It proved that so many people in her past were better than she was.

Anger and resentment had clung to her life since the moment she'd walked out on her grandmother. She'd lived her life selfishly. No wonder she was in debt and unhappy. Cutting the people you love out of your life never led to great things.

Glancing over at Blossom, she gave her a sheepish look. "I'm sorry," she whispered as she swiped at her cheeks.

Blossom shook her head. "We all heal differently. Your journey was different than mine. Trust me, I wasn't always this zen. I was angry when I woke up unable to walk. I was worried about my ability to take care of Isaac. He was my world, and I failed him."

Blossom gave Holly a sympathetic smile. "But people have a way of forgiving you even if you're not ready to ask for it."

Holly pinched her lips together as the image of her grandmother's face floated into her mind. Suddenly, all she could think about were the letters that were hidden upstairs in her room. "The letters."

Blossom nodded. "Yes…and Stephen." She ran her gaze over Holly and sighed. "He loves you, and he will fight for you until his dying breath, no matter what he says."

Holly swallowed as emotions rose up inside of her. It hurt to hear that. Not only because it meant what she suspected all along was true. That she didn't love Tyler—not like she loved Stephen. But it also meant she'd been mean to him. She'd hurt him.

And yet, she still didn't know what she was going to do about the inn or her debt.

"But don't you go giving him hope if there isn't any. Get your own house in order before you drag Stephen into it," Blossom said as she raised her finger.

Holly nodded and grabbed the door handle. Then, feeling sheepish, she turned to glance over at Blossom. "Are you going to be okay?"

Blossom nodded. "I'll be fine. I know how to find my way back to the reception desk."

Holly shot her a smile. "Thanks."

"You're welcome." Then a slow smile spread across her lips. "I'm impressed. Not many people make it through my speeches." She nodded. "I think you'll be great for Stephen."

Hope rose up inside of Holly as she made her way out into the hall. The urge to discover what her grandmother had hidden in those letters caused her to half walk, half run through the hall and up the stairs. At the top of the landing, she paused. She could hear Isaac and Stephen's laughter coming from the dining room. She'd snuck a peek of them decorating the last tree.

A smile spread across her lips as she made a beeline for her room. Once inside, she shut the door and turned, her gaze falling on the desk.

Sure, it was mostly hidden by the evergreens that dotted her room, but she knew it was there. Hiding behind the pine-scented mammoths was the thing she'd been avoiding since she got here.

Her grandmother.

Taking in a deep breath, she walked over to the desk and pulled open the drawer. Two envelopes stared back at her. Shaking, she reached in and pulled them out.

She clung to them as she turned and made her way over to her bed. Taking in a deep breath, she held them to her chest. She wasn't sure why. Maybe it was to prepare herself for whatever lay inside.

Was it the truth? More lies?

She swallowed as she located the first envelope. The one that Rex had handed her during his last reading of the will. She set the letter that Stephen had given her down on the mattress and turned her full attention to the envelope resting on her lap.

"It's just a letter. You can open a letter," she said out loud, feeling a little silly.

"Just like a bandage," she whispered as she slid her finger under the flap and began to tear. Just as she reached the end, there was a knock on the door.

She yelped and flung the letter down, whipping her gaze over to the door. Heat crept up her cheeks as she realized how ridiculous she'd just been. What had gotten into her?

The knock came again, so she stood and walked over. She opened the door to find Mrs. Brondy on the other side. She was holding...a letter. She was tapping it against her open hand.

When Holly met her gaze, she held out the letter. "For you," she said, wiggling it underneath Holly's nose.

Holly took the envelope. "Thanks," she said.

Mrs. Brondy nodded. Then she leaned in. "Hope said it was *in case of an emergency.*" Mrs. Brondy ran her gaze up and down Holly. "I think this qualifies." Then she dusted off her hands and made a beeline for the stairs.

Completely confused, Holly headed back into her room, shutting the door behind her. She glanced over at the two abandoned letters on the bed and then to the one in her hand.

"Thanks, Grandma," she said, tipping her eyes toward the ceiling. "Always have to make things complicated."

Ready to get this over with, Holly walked back over to the bed and finished tearing the first letter open.

Then she took in a deep breath and pulled out a single sheet of paper. It was folded into thirds—neatly creased on both sides.

She hesitated before slowly unfolding the letter.

She glanced down at her grandmother's perfect penmanship. Each letter flowed with exquisite grace. Tears filled her eyes as feelings, good and bad, rushed through her

She skimmed the letter, not really reading the words, just getting lost in the familiarity of her grandmother's writing. She used to watch her grandmother write, whether it was putting together a grocery list or writing down a booking for the inn.

It was like Hope's penmanship was a part of Holly that she'd forgotten a long time ago. And now that she was faced with it, it felt overwhelming.

She cleared her throat and focused her attention on what the words actually said.

My dearest Holly,

Words cannot describe how sorry I am that you are reading this. If you are, that means I've gone, and we haven't reconciled. I have failed you.

Holly blinked as her eyes filled with tears. She could feel the sorrow in her grandmother's words, and it matched her own.

Why had she been so selfish? Why had she stayed away for so long? Fighting what she already knew to be true. Christmas Inn would always have a special place in her heart.

I didn't say everything I wanted to the night you left. There was so much about your mother that would have hurt to utter out loud. I

wanted to be all you needed in your life. I know now that I was wrong. I shouldn't have kept her from you. I should have told you the truth.

Holly found herself nodding along as she read. It was true. Hope should have been open and honest. It hurt that her grandmother had spent Holly's entire childhood hiding things from her.

Your mother and I have a complex relationship. I put too much pressure on her, and she refused to take responsibility for the things that she did. When she became pregnant with you, I wasn't sure what to say or do.

I reacted badly. I didn't want her to miss out on her childhood. I wanted her to give you up for adoption.

Holly swallowed as she read the last words. Adoption. How different would her life be if her mom had actually done that?

I drove her away. She wouldn't give you up, so I threw her out of the house. She didn't speak to me for months. You were born, and she never called to tell me. It wasn't until you were a year old that she came to see me.

She couldn't take care of you. She left you in the foyer of the inn and disappeared.

I searched for her. I wanted to apologize, to move forward, but she'd vanished.

Holly's gaze softened as she realized that her grandmother's writing had become shaky. As if the words were painful for her to write. She could feel the anguish her grandmother felt, and it took her breath away.

I should have never placed you in that situation. I should have always been upfront and honest with you. It's what you deserved. But I feared how you would look at me if you learned why you were left. That it was my weakness that left you without a mother.

I loved you so much and I'd failed Lauren so much that if I lost you, too, I didn't think I could make it.

And yet, I lost you anyway.

Can you find it in your heart to forgive me? I don't want you to live your life like I did mine. Full of regret and anger.

Please understand that the reason I wanted you to return to Christmas Inn was because I knew how much it meant to you. Sometimes, it's easier to face your past if you have to.

I'm going to end this letter because I've just begun to ramble. If you've read this far, I'll take hope that there's a chance for reconciliation between us. Know I have and always will love you.

Love,

Your Grandmother

Holly stared at the letter as her grandmother's words sunk in around her. Exhaustion took over and she collapsed back onto the bed. She pulled the piece of paper onto her chest and hugged it.

She allowed regret and pain to wash over her. It was freeing, to allow herself to feel everything she'd been keeping herself from acknowledging.

Her grandmother taking responsibility for what happened helped. But Holly also realized that to err is human. Holly wasn't perfect, so why was she pretending that her grandmother needed to be?

She'd idolized her grandmother for so long, put unrealistic expectations on her that she could never fulfill. So when the truth came to light, finding out her grandmother wasn't perfect hurt almost as much as the facts about her mom.

Closing her eyes, Holly took in a deep breath and then let it out again. As she exhaled, all the tension she'd been holding onto for so long was expelled. It was cleansing, letting everything go. Accepting what happened and moving forward.

The only regret she had was that she hadn't reached out to her grandmother earlier. That she had waited for so long. And had Hope not passed away, forcing her to come to Christmas Inn, she might have never faced the demons that haunted her.

She wasn't sure how long she lay there, allowing the feeling of peace to come over her. But the memory of shirtless Stephen handing her an envelope came to her mind.

She sat up, wondering what her grandmother had written. She

glanced around, finding the letter and holding it in her hands. She turned it over and slide her finger under the flap.

Excitement rose up inside of her. What did Hope have to say now?

STEPHEN

Stephen stood in the laundry room, staring at the boxes of gifts in front of him. He growled as he unrolled some wrapping paper and then set one of the boxes on top of it. Reaching for the scissors, he opened them, pressed the spot where the blades joined against the edge of the paper and pushed.

The scissors took off, but he must have angled it wrong, because suddenly he wasn't cutting the paper, he was ripping it.

Exasperated, he threw the scissors down. He gripped the edge of the counter and hung his head, taking in a deep breath.

"Everything okay?" Blossom's voice asked from behind him.

Stephen tipped his head in her direction. She was half masked by his arm, but he didn't move. His thoughts were jumbled, and he felt so confused that he didn't have the energy to do the slightest task.

But Blossom looked expectant, so he sighed and straightened. "Why does gift wrapping have to be so complicated?" He raised the torn part of the paper to emphasize his words.

Blossom laughed as she rolled over to him. "Because you're not treating it delicately." She shifted the present over and grabbed the scissors.

Stephen watched as his sister cut the paper perfectly. Blossom looked triumphant as she turned to wave at the paper. "And that's how it's done."

Stephen sighed and rolled his eyes. "I'm not meant to wrap Christmas presents, apparently."

Blossom chuckled. "And yet, you run Christmas Inn…"

At the mention of the inn, Stephen's stomach twisted. He didn't want to think about that. All it led to was thoughts about Holly. And he didn't want to think about Holly.

He'd managed to avoid her all day. Which wasn't too hard because she ended up staying in her room for most of it. He busied himself with decorating and spending time with Isaac—but his mind kept wandering back to a place he didn't want it to go.

Last night and the kiss they shared.

"Oh no. I know that look. What happened?"

Stephen glanced over at his sister and shrugged as he started taping the paper. "I don't want to talk about it. It's not a big deal."

Blossom's brows went up. "What happened?" she asked again. He could tell she was going to keep asking until Stephen answered.

So he sighed and turned to face her. "I kissed Holly. She didn't kiss me back. End of story."

Blossom's jaw dropped. "You did what?"

Stephen hated how high Blossom's voice went. As if he'd just announced that he had shaved his eyebrows off. "It's not a big deal. I'm over it."

Blossom wheeled herself until she was in front of him. "Stephen, this is a big deal. She has a boyfriend."

Stephen cleared his throat. Those words felt like a vice around his chest. He blinked a few times, trying to force his body to calm down. There was no need to panic. He'd already come to terms with his mistake, no need to allow his sister to freak him out.

"I know. It was a mistake."

Blossom held his gaze, as if she were sizing him up. And then she sighed. "What are you going to do about it?"

Stephen sighed and turned to face his sister head on. Even though she was tiny, she didn't flinch. She folded her arms and stared at him.

"Nothing, okay? It was a mistake, it's over. We've both moved on." He scrubbed his face and then tipped it toward the ceiling. "She's selling the inn, and once that is over, we'll never see each other again." To emphasize how okay he was with this, he shot her a wink.

Blossom didn't look impressed. Instead she held her gaze steady for a moment before she blew out her breath and turned her attention back to the present.

"I can see why you're hiding out here, now."

Stephen returned to his sloppy taping job while throwing her an annoyed look. "I'm not hiding out. I'm wrapping presents. I don't want Isaac to see what I got him."

Blossom jutted a finger at the boxes. "All of these are for Isaac?"

Stephen held his arms out in an attempt to shield the presents from Blossom's view. "And some are for you." Then he narrowed his eyes. "But don't ask what I got you, because I'll never tell," he said, emphasizing the last two words.

Blossom stared at him and sighed. "You didn't have to buy me anything. You already take care of me. The scale between us is tipping more toward you than me."

Stephen chuckled as he leaned over and planted a kiss on her head. "It's because I love you more, that's why."

Blossom shot him an annoyed look. But just then, Holly's voice sounded from behind him.

Instantly, his heart picked up speed and his back straightened. His gaze landed on his sister to see that her eyes were wide as her gaze focused on Holly.

"Hey," Holly said, her voice quiet.

"Hey," Blossom said as she glanced over at Stephen.

He hoped that his furrowed brow and panicked expression made it clear to his sister that under no circumstances should she leave. But it didn't seem to register with her—or she was ignoring it.

Instead, she smiled at Holly. "I should go check the desk," she said as she wheeled past.

"Oh, okay," Holly said.

"Unless you wanted to talk to me, too?" Blossom said from behind Stephen.

He wanted to look, to see how Holly would react, but he didn't want to turn around. Instead, he stood there like an idiot, waiting to hear her response.

"Um, actually, I just need to talk to Stephen."

"I figured. Well, he's all yours."

Stephen's muscles felt as if they were going to spasm from how tense he was. If this was how the rest of his Christmas holiday was going to be, Holly couldn't leave fast enough. He was exhausted and ready for his life to settle down.

As Blossom left the room, it became very quiet. Stephen felt stupid for not wanting to turn around. He was a confident guy, but no matter what he told himself, he felt so out of sorts around Holly.

"Stephen," Holly's voice broke the silence.

His shoulders tightened and then relaxed. He took a deep breath and slowly turned. Holly was standing a few feet away. Her expression was soft, and he wasn't quite sure what to make of it.

He studied her. He could tell she was hurting, but he didn't know why. From what happened last night, he should be the broken one. No matter, though, he still loved her. He always would. And he didn't want to see her hurt. He wanted to her to be happy even if that meant he wasn't.

"What's wrong?" he asked, reaching out for her. But he stopped himself before he actually acted on his feelings.

Holly's gaze dropped down to his hand for a moment before she brought it back to meet his gaze. She swallowed and then held out a piece of paper that she was clutching. He took it, glancing down to see what she'd written.

On it was an address and a name: Lauren Graham.

He furrowed his brow. Was it possible? Was this Holly's mom?

"Is this—"

"Yes." Holly nodded. "I was wondering if you could take me there."

Stephen glanced down at the address. It was for Jamestown, which was about an hour drive from Ivy Springs.

"Tonight?" he asked. He'd take her in a heartbeat, but he had so many presents to wrap, and he was exhausted.

Holly chewed her bottom lip as she slowly began to nod. "If that's okay," she whispered.

He studied her. He could tell that she was going through something. Something deep. And he didn't want to her to be alone. If he didn't take her, would she call for a ride? And did he really want that person to be the one to console her?

Stephen folded the piece of paper back up and handed it to her. "Meet me out in the garage in five."

Holly slipped the paper into her back pocket and nodded. Then she paused and glanced up at him. Her eyes were full of gratitude. "Thank you," she said.

Stephen took that moment to glance down at her. To really take her in. She was so beautiful, even in the light of the laundry room. Her skin was pale, and he could see the soft splash of freckles across her nose. He could get lost in the depth of her blue eyes.

His gaze flicked down to her lips for a moment before he brought it back up, forcing all of those thoughts from his mind. He'd already acted on them, and he couldn't do it again.

"Of course. What are friends for?" he asked as he attempted to shrug off his feelings and head toward the door.

After slipping on his coat and boots, he made his way into the garage. Holly was already there. Her hand was on the door, and she looked as if she were in a trance.

Stephen walked up behind her. "Everything okay?" he asked.

Holly snapped her attention over to Stephen and nodded. But that nod slowly morphed into her shaking her head.

"No," she whispered.

Stephen stepped closer, hoping his presence wasn't unwelcome. When she didn't pull away, he decided to take that as a good sign.

He glanced down at the piece of paper that she had clutched in her hand. The handwriting looked familiar.

"May I?" he asked as he pulled gently on the paper.

Holly nodded and released it.

"Is this Hope's handwriting?"

Holly nodded slowly. "Yes. It's one of the letters she gave me."

He turned it over and over. "And this was it? This was in the envelope I gave you?"

Holly shook her head. "No. This wasn't the one you gave me. This was from Mrs. Brondy."

"Oh," he said. Then he furrowed his brow. "What did the one I gave you say?"

It may have been the poor lighting in the garage, but Stephen swore he saw Holly's cheeks flush pink. And suddenly, she was very interested in getting into the car.

"We should get going. I don't want to show up at my estranged mother's in the middle of the night."

Stephen parted his lips to protest, but at the desperate look in Holly's eyes, he closed his mouth.

He could ask another time. It looked like she wanted to battle one demon at a time. So he nodded and motioned toward the door. But Holly didn't seem to be waiting for his invitation—she was already pulling the door open.

Stephen walked over to the driver's side. After climbing in, he started the engine and waited as Holly buckled her seatbelt. Then she blew out her breath as she rested her head on the headrest behind her.

"Ready?" Stephen asked, just in case she wanted to call it quits and sprint back to the inn.

Holly didn't open her eyes. Instead she just nodded and muttered a soft, "yes."

Stephen put his truck into reverse and backed down the driveway. Once he was safely on the highway, he allowed himself to settle in. This was going to be a long drive, he might as well get comfortable.

HOLLY

Holly was a nervous wreck and seriously doubted her decision to get into Stephen's truck and drive to meet her mom.

Was she crazy? Why did she think this was a good idea?

Her mom had abandoned her. How was she going to feel when her daughter showed up on her doorstep the night before Christmas Eve? Groaning, Holly covered her face. This was a mistake. A huge, colossal mistake.

She should just tell Stephen to turn his truck around and drive her home. At least then, she'd be safe. Not entering into this world of the unknown.

Suddenly, Stephen's hand appeared in her line of sight. He grasped her fingers in his own and squeezed. The first thought she had was to pull away. To protect herself. To protect her heart. She was already entering into unknown territory, there was no need to add her feelings for Stephen into the mix.

But the longer she allowed him to hold her hand, the better it felt. It was like he knew exactly what she needed. He was there for her. In a way that was lacking in her life.

And then her thoughts returned to the letter that Hope had

written her. The one from Stephen. It had been simple and exactly what Holly needed to hear.

Forgive Stephen.

This wasn't his fault even though he's spent every day since you left fearing that it was.

He is loyal and good. He is exactly what you need in your life. If I could pick a man for you, I'd pick one that is so deeply in love with you, he doesn't know what to do with himself.

But I know you have your freedom to do what you want. Just, don't write him off.

Not yet.

Holly swallowed. She snuck a peek at Stephen, who was studying the road. She could see his tight jaw muscles under his five-o'clock shadow.

What her grandmother had said about him was true. He was perfect. From his loyalty to the inn and her grandmother to his love for Isaac and his sister. Wrap that up with his feelings for her, and Holly was pretty sure what she needed to do.

Tyler would never make her happy the way Stephen could. If she really wanted to be happy, then she needed to take charge of her life. She needed to forget the perfect life that she'd thought she wanted in New York. She needed to reevaluate what she was going to do once her trip to Ivy Springs was over.

Glancing down at his hand still wrapped around hers, she wondered if she would be able to walk away from him a second time. Would she be able to tell him goodbye?

Emotions rose up in her throat. No, she didn't think she had the strength. And the longer she was with him, the more she was beginning to realize that she didn't want to.

She didn't want to walk away from him ever again.

But then Blossom's words came to the forefront of her mind. *Get your own house in order before you drag Stephen into it.* Holly swallowed and slipped her hand out from under Stephen's. Blossom was right. Holly wasn't in a place where she could give her heart fully over to Stephen—even if she wanted to.

She needed to fix herself first. That's what Stephen deserved.

Stephen cleared his throat as he brought his hand back to the wheel. Then he shifted in his seat. She could tell he was agitated, and she hated that she was making him feel like that.

"Sorry," she whispered, not really sure if she wanted him to hear it. What was she going to say after that? Sorry I can't love you like I want to? How would that make him feel any better?

"What are you going to do once you meet your mom?" Stephen finally asked.

Holly glanced over at him. He wasn't asking about why she was sorry or about their relationship. It was a simple question about her.

"I don't know," she said. And that was the truth. She really didn't know what she was going to do or say. She just knew, the moment she read the address, that she needed to gather her courage and go.

She feared if she allowed herself to sleep on it, that she'd wake up tomorrow and her resolve would be gone. It was a now or never situation.

Stephen glanced over at her and shot her a smile. And then, in true Stephen fashion, he winked. That small gesture made her laugh. It felt incredible to open herself up to Stephen like this.

This entire trip to Ivy Springs had been so taxing on her. She was holding onto so much hurt and pain, and the simple laughter filled her soul.

When she finally stopped laughing, she glanced over to see Stephen sneaking a few glances her way. His smile had returned, and he looked like a kid on Christmas morning.

Holly blotted her eyes. "What?" she finally asked.

Stephen shrugged as he rested his wrist on the steering wheel. "I just haven't seen you laugh like that in a long time. It looks good on you."

Holly felt her cheeks warm as she pinched her lips together. It was sweet of Stephen to say that. And it was so true. It had been a long time since she'd laughed like that.

They kept their conversation light as they continued to drive. It was nice, just sitting there talking to Stephen. It helped her forget where she was headed and what she was about to do.

But unfortunately, it had to end. Stephen clicked on his blinker and took a left. They were suddenly on a dirt road. Holly bounced back-and-forth as he drove.

Everything felt more real as she realized they were no longer on the highway. The person at the end of this long road was going to be her mother.

The mother she'd been so desperate to see for so long. The mother she'd convinced herself she didn't care about. Who constantly lived in her past like a shadow she couldn't avoid.

How do you face a ghost from your past? What was she supposed to say? Did her mom even want her in her life?

It seemed that if she knew Holly lived an hour away, she would have attempted to see her at some point if that had been her desire.

Anxiety rose up in her chest and she began to feel as if an elephant was sitting on her, making it impossible to breathe. She didn't want Stephen to know how she was feeling, so she covered her mouth with her fingers. She was afraid of what she might do if she allowed this pain to consume her.

Stephen turned onto a driveway and they approached a small, yellow house. It was surrounded by snow-covered trees that glistened in the moonlight.

"I can't do this. I can't go up there. Slow down." Holly reached out and gripped Stephen's arm. It no longer mattered if she was touching him or not. She needed him to stop.

Thankfully, Stephen listened. He slowed down and pulled the truck off to the side, turning off the headlights. He waited for a moment, his gaze turned towards the house.

Feeling like an idiot, Holly buried her face in her hands. She'd dragged Stephen all the way out here just to chicken out a few hundred yards from the house.

This was supposed to be her grand gesture to both Stephen and her grandmother. And herself. This was going to be the proof that she had moved forward. That the letters and her time at the inn had given her the strength and courage to face the demons of her past.

But she didn't feel strong. She felt completely weak as she sat there trying to disappear into the fabric of her seat.

"Holly, it's okay. You don't have to go up there." Stephen's voice was low, and she could hear the emotion that coated his words.

Holly wanted to feel relieved at his words. She wanted to believe that if Stephen was okay with her not facing her mother, then she could be too. But it didn't help. She still felt frustrated and angry with herself.

The truth was if she told Stephen to turn around and take her home, she would always regret it. She would always wonder what would've happened had she gotten out of the car and knocked on the door.

She took a deep breath and glanced over at Stephen. Then she shook her head. "I'll never forgive myself if I don't go up there. I just need a moment."

Stephen was watching her, and as the last words left her lips, he slowly began to nod. "Okay," he said as he gripped the steering wheel with both hands and blew out his breath. "Then we'll wait till you're ready."

Holly took a moment to close her eyes and calm her mind. She thought of all the great things she might find on the other side of that door. And she allowed herself to feel confident in her decision. Reaching out to her mother was going to help her become the person she wanted to be.

As her resolve grew, she found her mood lightening. The unknown was scary, but she was going to be okay.

She had to have faith that her grandmother wouldn't send her to her mother's front door if she knew the experience would be negative. Her grandmother wouldn't send her into the lion's den unprepared.

Even though she and her grandmother had had their issues, the letters had said it all. Her grandmother loved her, and she loved her grandmother. And right now, that love extended to trust. Trust that her grandmother knew what she needed even if it was scary. That in the end, Holly would get exactly what she needed in her life. A mom.

After shushing her fears, she glanced over at Stephen. He was busy studying the steering wheel. She could tell that he had a lot on his mind. He was a busy man, and the fact that he'd chosen to be here with her meant everything.

It amazed her that no matter what, he was still here. He was the support she didn't know she was missing.

"I'm ready," she said, nodding toward the house.

He glanced over at her and then smiled. "Really?"

She returned his smile. "Really."

Stephen turned the lights back on and threw the truck into drive. He made it up the rest of the driveway and pulled into a little alcove. He glanced over at her as he turned off the engine. "Do you...?" he started to ask, his voice drifting off.

Holly nodded. "Yes, please." There was no way she wanted to be alone. If something bad did happen, she wanted him next to her to support her.

Stephen held her gaze for a moment and then he jumped out and slammed the door. Before she realized what he was doing, he'd jogged around and opened her door. He held out his hand. Holly paused then slipped her hand into his and allowed him to help her down.

As soon as her feet were on the ground, she knew that she

should pull her hand away. But she didn't want to. It felt right to hold his hand. When he didn't pull away, either, she took that as a good sign.

"Come on," she whispered as she started walking toward the front door.

Stephen kept in step with her. Their shoes crunched on the snow beneath them. The darkness was calming as they walked through it.

Holly took in a deep breath, drawing Stephen's attention. She watched from the corner of her eye as he studied her. Then he squeezed her fingers and leaned in.

"You'll do great," he said.

Holly nodded. "I hope so."

They climbed the three steps to the porch. And then she was standing at the front door, staring at it. She felt paralyzed. She knew she should knock, but she couldn't find the strength to lift her hand. Instead, she felt rooted to the spot, fear creeping into her mind again.

Stephen must have realized what was going on, so he did it for her. The knocks sounded on the door. The hollow thunks reverberated in her chest.

She held her breath as she waited for something to happen. Her ears were perked for the sound of someone on the other side.

The sound of a lock releasing caused her heart to pick up speed. Then the door handle turned. As the door opened, it revealed a woman standing on the other side.

Her hair was gray and pulled up into a bun at the top of her head. She looked like a younger version of Hope. Holly stared at her, wondering if this was real. Was this her mom?

"Yes?" the woman asked as she ran her gaze over Stephen and then Holly. When she met Holly's gaze, her face fell and her eyes filled with tears.

"Holly?" she whispered.

All of the emotions that were swirling around in Holly's body surged. A tear slid down her cheek as her mom stepped forward onto the porch. She was wearing a deep-red sweater and jeans.

"Is that you?" she asked, moving even closer to Holly.

"Mom?" Holly asked.

Lauren's gaze softened as she tipped her head to the side. "It's so good to see you," she said as she wrapped her arms around Holly and pulled her close. "I've missed you so much." Her voice was muffled by Holly's hair, but it didn't matter.

In the moment, in that hug, all of Holly's fears about what her mother would say or how she would feel when she came face to face with the woman who'd left her, all faded away.

This was what she needed this Christmas season. To be reunited with someone she thought was gone from her life forever.

Lauren pulled away as she smiled at Holly. "Come on, come inside, it's freezing out here. I'll make a pot of coffee and we can talk."

Holly nodded and began to follow after Lauren, who paused and glanced over at Stephen.

"And you are?" she asked, extending her hand.

Stephen cleared his throat and glanced at Holly, as if he were waiting for her to answer for him.

Holly smiled. "This is Stephen. He's my very good friend."

Stephen raised his eyebrows and then met Lauren's hand. They shook and Lauren nodded.

"It's nice to meet you, Stephen. Come on in as well. I could use the company."

They followed Lauren into the house. She shut the door behind them and then waved toward the kitchen. "I think I've got some cookies in the pantry," she said as she stepped around a very furry white cat that was sleeping on the floor.

"It's okay if you don't," Holly said as she pulled her shoes off and then headed after her. Holly could hear Stephen's footsteps as he followed.

When they got to the kitchen, Lauren was filling a coffee pot with water. After she got it started, she turned and motioned toward the table. "Come. Sit. I'm sure we've got a lot to talk about."

Holly nodded and made her way to the table, where she pulled out a chair. Once they were all seated, Lauren spoke up.

"Go ahead and ask me any question you want. I'm not shy."

Holly sat up straighter in her chair and met Lauren's gaze. "All right," she said. Even though she knew this was going to be a touchy conversation, she was okay with that. After all, if she wanted her mom in her life, she was going to have to fight for that relationship.

She wasn't going to lose another person she loved because she was scared. Right now, she was going to stand up and be brave.

HOLLY

Holly woke up the next morning feeling lighter than she had in a very long time. She stretched out on her bed and took in a deep breath. After holding it for a few seconds, she released it and opened her eyes.

Her conversation with her mom went well into the night. They talked a lot about Hope and what had happened. Her grandmother had reached out to her mom a few months ago. Hope had been tired of living a life of regret.

It took a while, but they reconciled.

Holly tried not to cry, but it had been in vain. There were many points in their conversation when both women were in tears, hugging each other.

But at two in the morning, Holly declared that it was time to go, and she and Stephen left.

The entire time they were at Lauren's, Stephen was quiet. He kept his arms folded and just listened as the two of them talked.

It was nice, having him next to her. She could feel his support and knew if she needed him, he would be there for her. It was a feeling she hadn't had in a long time, and she hated to admit it, but she didn't feel that with Tyler.

It was time for her to do something about that.

Grabbing at the nightstand, she found her phone. After blinking a few times to adjust her eyes, she located Tyler's cell number and pressed, hoping he would have cell service. She turned to her side while she held the phone to her ear and waited. It felt like forever before Tyler picked up.

"Hey," he said. His voice was low, like he'd been sleeping.

"I'm sorry, did I wake you?" Holly glanced at the clock. It was nine in the morning, but she had no clue what time it was for him.

"I, um...not really," he finally said.

Holly nodded as she pushed herself up into a sitting position. She drew her feet toward her and rested her head on her knees. She hated that she was going to break up with him over the phone, but it wasn't like she had any other option.

"I think we need to talk," she said, her voice low.

Tyler cleared his throat. "Yeah, I need to talk to you too."

Holly raised her eyebrows. "Is everything okay?"

Silence.

"Holly, I'm not going to lie to you. I met someone," Tyler said at a speed that matched her pounding heart.

Holly couldn't help the smile that spread across her lips. "You did?" This was perfect. She didn't want to hurt Tyler, and if he'd found someone else, it meant she wasn't going to.

He sighed. She could picture his slumped shoulders and down-turned lips. "I didn't mean to. She's a nurse stationed with us. It kind of...just happened."

Holly realized that he felt bad. Like really bad. And she didn't want him to. Not when she was actually really happy for him.

"It's okay, Tyler. I don't blame you." She let out her breath slowly as she contemplated what to say next. "I don't think we were going to last forever. We want different things."

Tyler paused. She could feel his hesitation in his voice. "The inn?" he asked.

Holly nodded as she closed her eyes. There was no way Tyler

would ever want to move to Ivy Springs. He was a city guy, and even though she spent her entire time in New York trying to convince herself otherwise, she was a country girl.

Sure, she didn't know what she was going to do about her debt. And she wasn't sure how she was going to run the inn. But she knew she couldn't sell this place. And she couldn't leave Stephen. Not again.

"I'm staying here," she said.

"I'm happy for you, Hol. I'm happy you found what you've been looking for."

Holly furrowed her brow. "I've been looking for something?"

Tyler chuckled. "Yeah. You've never fully committed to anything. Your designs. Us." Then he hurried to say, "I'm not complaining, just making an observation. If going to Christmas Inn was what you needed to rediscover what you've been missing, then I'm happy for you."

Tears brimmed Holly's eyes as she nodded. He was right. Ever since she left Ivy Springs, nothing had felt complete. Now, she was back home, and even though her grandmother wasn't here, she had her mom. Or at least, the start of a relationship she'd been wanting her whole life.

"You'll be okay?" she asked.

Tyler laughed. "I'll be great. I actually love working for Doctors Without Borders. I think it might be my calling. I'm going to stay on for a while."

Holly smiled. "You're going to do great. They're lucky to have you."

"Thanks, Holly."

Holly took in a deep breath as she nodded. "Well, I should probably go. I've got a ton of things to do to get ready for Christmas Eve."

"All right. Have a great Christmas, Holly Graham."

"Have a great life, Tyler Potter."

"I plan to."

The call ended, so Holly pulled the phone from her ear and turned off the screen. She set the phone next to her on the bed as she flopped onto her back and stared up at the ceiling.

She took a few deep breaths as she realized just how free she felt. Smiling, she threw her blankets off and stood. After a long, hot shower, she dressed and picked up her phone.

Last night, she and Lauren had made plans to do some Christmas shopping today. When she located her mom's phone number, she texted her.

Holly: I'm up and dressed. Whenever you're ready, I'll be here.

Lauren: I'm already on my way. I'll be there in 15.

Holly smiled as she slipped her phone into her purse and grabbed her shoes. After tying the laces, she stood and wandered over to the Christmas trees.

This was the first time in a long time that she'd welcomed the sight of anything having to do with Christmas. The excitement of the holiday season once again burned within her.

She was going to make this Christmas the best Christmas ever. After all, she had quite a few to make up for.

After throwing on her coat, she made her way down the stairs to the foyer. Isaac was standing in front of the fireplace in the living room, staring at something.

Holly laughed as she walked over to him and crouched down. "What are you doing?" she asked.

Isaac glanced over at her as he adjusted an empty plate he'd set on the hearth. "I'm trying to figure out the best place to set Santa's cookies." He scrunched up his nose and then stuck out his tongue as if he were trying to get the angle just right.

Holly wrapped her arm around his shoulders and squeezed. "I'm sure Santa will love whatever you pick."

Isaac glanced over at her. Then he shook his head. "Nope. I need to get it just right."

Holly chuckled as she straightened. Movement by the reception desk drew her attention. Blossom was sitting behind the desk, and Stephen had just walked up next to her.

They were talking, and Holly took a moment to study Stephen. It felt good to finally acknowledge how good-looking he was. She knew she'd been an idiot to leave him. And there was no way that she was going to leave him again.

As if he sensed her looking at him, he glanced over and met her gaze. Embarrassed, she dropped her eyes and quickened her steps as she walked past them into the dining room.

She grabbed a plate with some pancakes and eggs. Then she poured herself a mug of coffee and found a table. She needed to eat fast before Lauren got here.

When she felt enough time had passed, she peeked over at Stephen again, just to see what he was doing. His attention was back on Blossom as she spoke in hushed tones.

Halfway through her breakfast, Lauren showed up. Holly swallowed her current bite and chased it down with a gulp of coffee. She stood and grabbed her purse as she waved toward Lauren, who didn't seem to notice her. Instead, she was making a beeline for Stephen.

"I'm ready," she said as she approached her mom.

Lauren turned and smiled. "Oh, good." Then she glanced back at Stephen. "Well, I guess we are off. It was good to see you again."

Stephen furrowed his brow as he looked at Holly. "Where are you going?"

Holly's cheeks heated from his gaze. Her stomach twisted with excitement. She was looking forward to telling him that she planned on staying at Christmas Inn, but she wanted to do it right.

"We're spending the day together," she said as she hooked arms with Lauren and began to pull her toward the door.

Lauren laughed as she waved at Stephen and Blossom. Once they were outside, with the door securely shut behind them, Lauren glanced over at her.

"Everything okay?" she asked as they walked down the porch steps and over to Lauren's car.

Holly blew out her breath as she stepped closer to her mom. It felt good, having someone to depend on. "Yes. I just needed to get out of there."

Lauren removed her key fob from her jacket pocket and unlocked the doors. "Get away from Stephen?"

Holly nodded as she slipped into the passenger seat and shut the door. Lauren walked around the hood to the driver's side. After she was situated with her seatbelt buckled, she turned to study Holly. "Anything I should know about?"

Holly shrugged. "I'm going to tell him I love him tonight."

Lauren's expression softened. "You are?"

Holly nodded. "Yes. But I have to prove to him first that I'm no longer Ms. Grinch."

Lauren put her car in reverse and pulled out of her parking spot. "Ms. Grinch?"

"That's the lovely nickname that Stephen and Isaac gave me."

"Isaac?"

"Stephen's nephew."

Lauren paused before she pushed the car into drive. Holly glanced over to see that her mom was staring at her with a soft smile on her lips.

"What?" she asked, not sure if her heart could take all the feelings that were coursing through her.

Lauren shrugged as she pressed on the gas. "I'm just happy you came to find me. It means a lot."

Holly smiled as she nodded. "I'm happy, too."

Lauren flicked her gaze over to Holly for a moment as she sped onto the highway. "Let's go get your guy," she said with laughter in her voice.

Holly's heart was pounding as she nodded. That was her intention.

STEPHEN

Christmas Eve dinner was amazing. Mrs. Brondy truly outdid herself. There was a turkey and a ham. Homemade cranberry sauce and fresh mashed potatoes. The rolls were divine, especially when they were slathered in her garlic herb butter.

Stephen couldn't eat another bite when he set his fork and knife down next to his plate and leaned back, allowing his stomach to expand.

"That was amazing," Blossom said.

Isaac was even staying in his seat as he sat next to Stephen, stuffing his face.

"Mrs. Brondy is a miracle worker."

Blossom chuckled. "Yeah. It's a pity she's going to have to find another job," Blossom said, glancing over at Stephen.

Stephen sighed as he scrubbed his face. It was true. Nothing he did had changed anything. The future was still set, and Blossom knew it. He should have just listened to her from the get-go.

No matter what he did, Holly would still sell Christmas Inn and go back to her boyfriend.

Holly seemed pretty content sitting next to her mom. They

were smiling and talking as if the fate of the inn—and their liveli-hood—wasn't in Holly's hands.

Why was she so calm? Didn't she understand what she was doing to every one of the customers in the dining room right now? Christmas Inn was an institution here in Ivy Springs, and selling it was dishonoring the memory of everyone who stayed here—who made memories here.

"Your face is turning red," Blossom said, snapping Stephen's attention over to her.

Stephen cleared his throat and calmed his mind. Then he glanced over at his sister. "It is not."

Blossom was mid-drink, so she just nodded.

"I'm full. Can I go?" Isaac asked. He was already off his chair and standing next to Stephen.

"Yeah," Stephen said before Blossom could respond.

Blossom swallowed her water quickly and parted her lips to speak, but Isaac was already gone.

"I hate it when you do that," she said as she stabbed a piece of ham with her fork and glared at Stephen.

He sighed, his gaze already making its way over to Holly once more. "Do what?"

"Parent him. I'm here. I'm his mom. I should be the one to excuse him."

Stephen scoffed as he turned to face his sister. But when he saw her hurt expression, he nodded. "Right. Sorry. I'll remember for next time."

She eyed him, and then a soft smile spread across her lips. "It's okay. If it wasn't for you, we wouldn't be here."

Stephen gave her a smile and then leaned in and kissed her cheek. "You're my sister. Where else would you go?" he asked as he scooted his chair out. "I'm going to check on Mrs. Brondy," he said as he grabbed his plate and brought it over to the pile of dishes stacked by the far wall.

Blossom nodded and returned to eating.

Stephen cleared his throat as he walked through the swinging kitchen door. Right before the door swung closed, he stole a glance at Holly. His heart began to pound as he caught her studying him. But then the door closed fully, shutting her off from him.

He blew out his breath and turned to find Mrs. Brondy standing next to the oven with a roll held between her lips. She was busy opening up the oven door and peeking in at the rolls inside.

"Go sit down," Stephen ordered as he shooed her away from the oven.

Mrs. Brondy mumbled something, but the roll muffled her words so Stephen couldn't make out what she was trying to say.

"I've got this. You go sit down and eat with everyone else." He grabbed the oven mitts from her which allowed her to remove the roll from her mouth.

"It's okay. I really should—"

"I wasn't asking. It's your Christmas, too." He narrowed his eyes as he tipped his head toward the door.

Mrs. Brondy held his gaze and then sighed as she grabbed her plate. "Five more minutes and they can come out," she said as she pressed her back to the door.

Stephen nodded and then moved to stand in front of the oven. He crouched down and peeked in through the glass door. Then sighing, he stood. And just as he turned around, he yelped.

Standing behind him like some stealth ninja was Holly.

Her eyes widened, and she raised her hands as if she were surrendering. "I'm so sorry. I didn't mean to scare you," she said as her cheeks flushed.

Stephen narrowed his eyes but then shook his head. "It's okay. I'm fine."

His heart was breaking just looking at her, so he turned and rested both hands on the counter. He tipped his head forward and took a deep breath. The day Holly left couldn't come fast enough. He wasn't sure how he was going to survive the next few days.

"How're things with your mom?" he asked.

"Great. We've been doing a lot of talking. We have a lot to catch up on."

He glanced over to see that Holly had moved to lean her hip against the counter across from him. Feeling like an idiot for trying to hide out in his own little world, he straightened and folded his arms.

It was a sort of standoff between the two of them. He swallowed as he looked at her. "When do you head back to New York? It's going to be hard to keep up a relationship with your mom being so far away."

Holly chewed on her bottom lip as she nodded. Then, her gaze met his, and it took his breath away. She looked so small, so broken. Like she wanted to say something but wasn't sure how.

"I wanted to give you this," she said as she reached behind her and pulled out a small envelope. She held it out toward him.

He furrowed his brow as he took it. "What is it?" he asked.

"Just open it."

Confused, Stephen slid his finger under the flap and tore at the paper. "A letter? Is this from Hope?"

Holly was studying him when he raised his gaze up to meet hers. She shook her head. "It's from me."

Intrigued and a little scared, Stephen opened the envelope the rest of the way. He removed a folded piece of paper and then set the ripped envelope on the counter next to him.

He unfolded the first flap and then the second. He stared at the first page of the deed for the inn. Stuck to the front was a neon pink Post-it note with the words *I'm sorry* written across it.

Frustration rose up inside of him. "You're selling?" he asked. Up until now, he'd hung onto the hope—though he'd never admit it—that Holly just might not sell this place.

"What?" she asked, stepping up to him and pulling down a

corner of the piece of paper. "No, that's not what I meant." Her face was flushed as she glanced up at him.

"You're *not* selling the inn?" he asked.

She shook her head. "No. I'm not."

Totally confused, he stared at her. "Then why did you say you were sorry?"

She studied him, and he could see the frustration in her gaze. "I was trying to tell you that I was sorry *and* that I'm *not* selling the inn."

He furrowed his brow and tried to process what she was saying. "You're really not selling the inn?"

She chewed her bottom lip as she shook her head. "How can I sell the place the means so much to me." She glanced up at him as if she were unsure of what he was going to say to that.

Realizing that his desperate hope was actually being realized, Stephen stepped forward. "And what does your boyfriend think of this?" He needed to know if she was still attached. If she wasn't, there wasn't a whole lot that was going to stand in his way. She was going to be his.

Holly shrugged. "He doesn't care. Not when he has his new girlfriend."

Stephen paused, rage rising up inside of him. "His what?"

Holly's hand rested on his forearm as she moved closer. "It's okay. I was actually going to break up with him. There's, someone else..." She let the last word linger as she glanced up at him.

They were standing inches apart now. Stephen could feel the heat of her body. All he wanted to do was reach for her. To pull her against him and never let her go.

But he wanted to make sure she was okay. That her heart wasn't broken from the prick that cheated on her. "Do you need me to talk to him?" he asked, making sure that his voice sounded gruff.

Holly laughed. It was soft and filled his soul. "No. I'm okay."

His hand slipped around her waist as he stepped closer. Holly had to tip her head all the way back so she could look up at him. She rested her hands on his arms and then slid them up, leaving a trail of shivers in their wake.

He growled as he dipped down, ready to press his lips to hers. Just before their lips touched, the timer rang.

He cursed under his breath as he glanced behind him. Then he turned back to give Holly a stern look. "Don't move," he growled as he dropped his hand and yanked open the oven.

Holly laughed, but Stephen was on a mission. He grabbed an oven mitt and then pulled the rolls from the oven and set them—thunk—down on the counter. He threw down the oven mitt and didn't even bother to close the oven. He had one thing on his mind and one thing only.

Holly.

He whipped around and placed both hands on her waist. He lifted her up onto the counter behind them and wrapped his arms around her. He pulled her so close to him, there was no way she was ever going to leave again.

His lips found hers. A sensation that he hadn't thought he could feel again coursed through his body. His lips moved against hers as if she held the answers to all the questions he wanted to ask.

Her hands wrapped themselves in his hair as she brought him closer. She parted her lips and let him in.

He growled as he deepened his kiss. He was never, ever going to let her go. She was his, and he was hers. It was how it had always been, and they were fools to think anything had changed.

When they were out of breath, Stephen pulled back to study her. Her gaze was hazy as she stared back at him. He tipped his forehead toward hers until they were touching.

He closed his eyes and allowed his heart to open. To let her in and love her wholly and completely.

"I love you, Holly Graham," he said as he pulled back so he could get lost in her eyes.

Tears brimmed her lids as she smiled at him. He leaned forward and pressed a kiss to her cheeks, the tip of her nose, her forehead, and then ended on her lips.

She giggled as she pulled back. "Hang on, I need to say it too."

He quirked an eyebrow. "You don't have to say it just 'cause I did."

She reached up and cradled his cheek in her hand. "I want to. I want you to know it."

He nodded as he reluctantly pulled back. "Okay, I'm ready."

She held his gaze, her expression turning serious. "I love you, Stephen. I always have. And even though our future is unknown, I wouldn't have it any other way."

His heart filled with so much love. So much complete and utter affection for the woman in front of him, that he pressed his lips to hers. Just so she knew what he felt for her.

Everything.

He didn't care that they didn't know what was going to happen in the future. He was sure they had a lot to talk about. But right now, it didn't matter. Not when he loved her as much as he did.

He was sure, no matter what, they would find a way. Because they would be together. And that was all that mattered.

EPILOGUE

Blossom

Christmas morning came too fast.

Blossom had spent half the night wrapping presents for Isaac. She'd spent so long trying to find the perfect gifts to make the holiday special for him.

She felt like such a failure that making him smile on Christmas day seemed like a small consolation. If she could make his holiday joyous, she would.

But right now, with Isaac bouncing on her bed, chanting for her to wake up, she was feeling less than jovial.

"Ike, dude, you're going to hurt yourself," she said as she rolled to her side to give him more room.

"Wake up! Wake up! Uncle Steppan said I can't open my presents until you're awake." Isaac dropped to his knees and peered over at Blossom. "He's making kissy faces with Ms. Grinch." Isaac made a "blech" sound and then stuck out his tongue.

Blossom laughed although, deep down inside, she was hurting. Hurting from the fact that she was going to have to watch as her brother made his perfect life with his perfect bride.

She would have to take Isaac away from the only home he'd ever known so that Stephen could have the life he deserved. And he really did deserve it, but she couldn't help the self-pity that rose up inside of her.

Not wanting to dampen the holiday spirit with her thoughts of doom and gloom, Blossom pulled the covers off her lap and glanced over at Isaac. "Get Mommy's wheelchair?" she asked.

Isaac's face lit up. "Can I ride in it?"

Blossom smiled as she nodded. "This once."

While Isaac was getting her chair, she worked on moving her legs off the side of the bed. Isaac had fun, surfing around the room in her wheelchair. He was getting just as good as she was at maneuvering around.

Even though it had been four years since the accident, she was still getting used to her new normal. She wasn't sure she ever was going to truly get used to it.

Finally, she had to call Isaac over. He groaned but obeyed. Soon, she was in her chair with a blanket draped over her legs.

Isaac lead the way, opening the door wide enough so she could fit through. The inn was alive with voices and the smell of pancakes and bacon. Blossom's stomach grumbled as she wheeled into the dining room. Stephen and Holly were snuggling, their chairs about as close as they could get to each other.

Blossom thought about sitting at a different table, but Stephen waved her over.

Sighing, Blossom forced a smile. This was going to be torture.

Sure, love still existed for others, she knew that, but she didn't want it shoved in her face. Not when she had written romance out of her life.

How could someone love her when she was confined to a chair? How could she ask anyone to take that on? Being a single mom was one thing. But being a mom in a wheelchair?

She mentally shook her head. These kinds of thoughts only sent her spiraling, and she couldn't do that to Isaac anymore. He deserved the best mom, and she was determined to be that for him.

"Sleep good?" Stephen asked as he stabbed his eggs with his fork.

Blossom nodded. "You?"

Stephen glanced over at Holly, and they both busted up laughing. Blossom didn't push for details. She wrinkled her nose and reached for the coffee pot so she could fill her mug.

"Let me," Holly said as she stood up and poured the coffee.

Blossom shot her a thankful smile, which Holly returned. "Can I get you a plate too?" Holly asked after she set the mug in front of Blossom.

Blossom nodded. "Thanks."

Holly made a beeline for the buffet. Blossom turned to see Stephen grinning at his pancakes like a fool.

"You are so in trouble," She said as she sipped at her coffee.

Stephen furrowed his brow. "What are you talking about?"

Blossom set down her mug and motioned to his face. "You're grinning like an idiot."

Stephen shrugged. "I'm happy. Holly makes me happy." He smiled again while he tipped his mug to his lips and took a drink.

Blossom wrinkled her nose and shook her head. "I'm happy for you."

"You definitely look it," he said, sarcasm dripping from his words.

Blossom shot him a *don't get started with me* look. "I can be happy for you and still be cynical about love."

Stephen furrowed his brows as he leaned in. He was seconds from telling her how great she was and how the right guy was just around the corner, so Blossom beat him to it.

"I'm okay. I've got Isaac. I don't need"—she waved her hand in front of his face—"that."

Stephen straightened as he pressed his hand to his chest. "You mean me? A brother who cares about his sister? You don't need me?"

Blossom shot him a look but couldn't fight the smile that formed on her lips. She loved her brother—even if he was naive. There weren't too many guys clamoring for a woman in her situation. She'd come to grips with that, and she would just have to wait for her brother to do the same.

Holly came back to the table with an overloaded plate. Thankfully, she distracted Stephen, which meant Blossom would have a few minutes of uninterrupted time to herself.

She dropped her gaze to her plate and pushed around the pancakes and eggs. She could hear Stephen and Holly laughing and whispering next to her. Her heart ached for something similar, but reality smacked her in the face.

She'd already accepted her future. Why was she fighting it now?

Stephen and Holly had issues, sure, but they were temporary. For Blossom, this wheelchair was her future. It wasn't an inn or some debt. It was her life.

And she knew that if *she* was having a hard time accepting what had happened to her, some random guy wouldn't do any better.

She was broken. End of story. It was foolish to dream that she would find someone someday. Dreaming brought pain, and she was hurting enough already.

Love wasn't in the cards.

***

If you're in the mood for MORE Christmas romance, head on over to Amazon and grab them ALL!
Christmasland
HERE
Second Chance Mistletoe Kisses

HERE
Forgiving the Billionaire
HERE

If you want more Ivy Springs Romance, grab your copy of
Summer at Christmas Inn TODAY!
Find out if Blossom finds love!
Grab it HERE!

Anne-Marie also has a fabulous Family Saga series.
Start book 1, Coming Home to Honey Grove,
HERE!

Join my Newsletter!
Find great deals on my books and other sweet romance!
Get, Fighting Love for the Cowboy FREE
just for signing up!
Grab it HERE!

SHE'S AN IRS AUDITOR DESPERATE TO PROVE HERSELF.
HE'S A COWBOY TRYING TO HOLD ONTO HIS RANCH.
LOVE WAS NOT ON THE AGENDA.

If you want to connect with Anne-Marie, head on over to website
for a list of her books.
HERE

She's love to connect with you on her social media platforms:

Facebook
Instagram

Made in the USA
Monee, IL
19 December 2020

54790827R00100